KITTEN HEELS

Allie,
I hope you
Enjoy your
Read!

Kryp

KRYS KING

KITTEN HEELS

Copyright © 2024 by Krystalynne King

All rights reserved.

No part of this book may be reproduced in any form or by any electronic or mechanical means including information storage and retrieval systems, without permission in writing from the author. The only exception is by a reviewer, who may quote short excerpts in a review.

This book is a work of fiction. Names, characters, places, and incidents either are products of the author's imagination or are used fictitiously. Any resemblance to actual persons, living or dead, events, or locales is entirely coincidental.

Published by The Writer's Alliance, LLC

ISBN: 979-8-9923052-1-0

Cover design & illustration: Mark Thomas / Coverness.com

To my family, whose unwavering love and support anchor me in every storm,

To my friends, who inspire me with their encouragement and laughter,

And to my readers, whose anticipation fuels my passion

and whose loyalty humbles me.

This book is for all of you—thank you for being part of this journey.

PRELUDE

"Thank you all for coming out today in support of the Found Voices Foundation. It means a lot not only to me but to everyone who has been a victim of molestation and rape; and those big checks you're about to write will mean even more."

The crowd laughs politely, the tension in the room softening just enough for me to feel in control. My words land perfectly—calculated but heartfelt. This is the first fundraiser I've thrown since establishing my foundation. Found Voices helps women reclaim their lives: therapy, essentials, schooling, job placement, housing—we've got it all. But for me, it's more than just that. This foundation isn't just about giving others their voice back; it's about reclaiming my own.

For years, I'd hidden behind walls so thick, even I forgot who I was. Raul broke those walls down. These days, I've let go of my ATMs, leaned into this softer life, and let him take the reins financially. Sure, I'm surprised he hasn't cracked under the pressure of funding me—but he's held his own. Diamonds, handbags, furs—he's kept me laced. And that new Mercedes he stunned me with this morning? That man knows how to keep me happy.

I glance out into the crowd and spot him standing in the corner. His glass catches the light as he lifts it toward me with a glistening smile. I grin back, my confidence radiating. Right now, I'm happy. With my life. With this man. And yes, with his money. Let's not get it twisted.

Clearing my throat, I return my focus to the audience. "No, but in all seriousness, starting Found Voices wasn't just about helping other women. It was about finding my own voice, the one that was taken from me by someone I trusted most—my father. Instead of protecting me, he silenced me, and I was alone for a long time. I became tough, untouchable, because I thought I didn't need anyone. But I did. And there are so many little girls and women out there who are exactly where I was. With your help, we can show them they're not alone. That their voices matter. That we're here to listen."

The applause rises, and I catch a few tears being dabbed in the audience. A tear slips down my own cheek, but I swipe it away quickly. Vulnerability is fine, but I'm still Mickey fucking Collins.

I step down from the stage, lifting the hem of my Halston Heritage gown slightly, and weave through the crowd toward Raul. Before I can reach him, an older woman stops me.

"Wonderful speech, Ms. Collins. What you're doing is spectacular."

"Thank you. You being here makes you just as spec—"

The room goes silent. A ripple of unease spreads as the

crowd parts like the Red Sea. The live band halts abruptly. Then I see them: hordes of FBI agents storming through, their badges flashing and their hands on holsters. My heart drops.

"What the hell is this?" I yell, storming toward the head agent. My ghetto side has stayed locked up all day, but let's be clear: nobody messes up my event without an explanation.

"Mickey Collins?" the agent asks, his tone sharp and impersonal.

"Yeah, that's me. Now tell me why the hell you're busting into my shit, causing a scene?"

"Mickey Collins, you're under arrest for money laundering, fraud, and identity theft."

"What?!"

He grabs my arm to cuff me, but I snatch loose. "What are you talking about?"

"Please do not resist," he warns, grabbing me again. The cold steel of handcuffs snaps around my wrists. "You have the right to remain silent. Anything you say…"

His voice fades. All I hear is the clank of the cuffs and my own pulse pounding in my ears. My eyes dart around the room, searching frantically for Raul. But he's nowhere. My chest tightens.

"Raul!" I scream, twisting to look behind me. "Raul!"

Nothing.

"That motherfucking bastard!" I yell as they drag me away. The last thing I see is the shocked faces of my donors and the sparkling chandelier above, mocking me.

PROLOGUE

The smell of stale cigarettes and despair clung to me as I sat in the cold steel chair at ACS, staring at the scuffed tile floor beneath my feet. My heel tapped nervously against the chair leg, a rhythm that matched the unease roiling in my chest. How did I end up here, waiting for a father I never knew?

Do you ever wonder if someone, somewhere, has lived through what you have? Experienced even a fraction of it? Surely, in a world this vast, there must be at least one other person who understands.

If not, then what had I done in my fourteen years to deserve this? ACS? Really?

"Did you hear me, Mikayla?"

The social worker—what was her name again?—snapped me out of my thoughts. She gave me a practiced smile—the kind that said she cared, or at least wanted me to think she did. But her disheveled appearance told a different story: frizzy synthetic weave, a wrinkled button-up shirt that barely hid her sloppily fitting khaki pants, and eyes heavy with the weight of too many cases just like mine. Her exterior screamed of someone worn thin by their own life, not mine. Why should I believe she cares about me when she can't even care for herself?

"We were able to contact your father. He's agreed to take you into his custody," she said, her smile widening as if expecting me to share in her relief.

My father? The word felt foreign, hollow. I hadn't heard my mom mention him once in my fourteen years of existence. He wasn't real to me, just a phantom whose sudden arrival in my life felt like some cruel cosmic joke.

"Did you hear me, sweetheart? Everything will be okay. Your dad will be here shortly."

Sweetheart? Okay? Dad? It's too much. I stand abruptly, the chair screeching against the tile.

"Where are you going?" she calls after me.

"As far away as possible," I muttered, brushing past her without a backward glance.

The guards at the door won't let me out, so I settle for the lobby; the place where kids like me waited for a fresh start that felt more like a punishment. I pressed my forehead against the cool glass of the window, watching cars zip across the expressway. I imagined myself in one of them, speeding toward the ocean, where the sun always shone and the water sparkled like freedom. But dreams like that didn't belong to girls like me. They were smothered by the smog of a life I hadn't chosen but was forced to survive.

My mom, Harriet Finley, or Love, as she was known on the streets, was the reason I was sitting at ACS. Love wasn't just a nickname; it was her whole identity, wrapped up in empty promises and broken dreams. To me, she was just my mother—a crack addict who had traded away her soul for the next hit. She used to be someone else, someone I could almost love, but the memories of who she was before the addiction were fading, smothered by years of neglect and chaos.

Last night, though—last night was the final straw.

The lights were out, the fridge was empty, and eviction loomed over us like a storm cloud ready to burst. Love had run out of options, or so she claimed. Her desperation took a new shape when she handed me over to him. There was no hesitation in her eyes, no flicker of shame. She'd made the exchange so easily, it sickened me.

The man reached for me, his hands rough and insistent. Fear surged through me, a burning wave that turned into rage. Before he could tighten his grip, I hit him with everything I had—a right hook Marv had taught me during one of our impromptu boxing lessons. The man staggered back, and I ran, my legs carrying me as far away as they could. I didn't stop until I collided with a tall figure in a police uniform.

Whoa, slow down," the man said, gripping my shoulders. He crouched slightly, bringing his face level with mine. "What's the rush?"

I swallowed hard, my pulse pounding in my ears. "Just on my way home," I mumbled, avoiding his gaze, pulling my arms from his grip and stepping back. My plan had been to head to Carmen's—my safe haven when home became unbearable.

"Where's home?" he asked, his voice calm but probing.

"155th." I responded pulling my arms from his grip and stepping backwards. I still do not know why I told him the truth to that question. It's never a good thing when you see a white cop in a black neighborhood, but he had kind eyes. Something about those eyes made me want to believe he wasn't like the others.

"You're going the wrong way, where are you coming from?" He asked as he straightened his stance and slid his hands into his pockets. I could tell he was waiting for me to lie. He knew I was running from something or someone.

Realizing his question was going to go unanswered, "Let me take you home." he said, gesturing toward his patrol car.

"I'm not getting into your car! I don't know you." I yelled, pushing past him, trying to escape the second man of the night.

"Oh no you don't." He stopped me. "We don't have to drive; I'll walk you home. Come on, let's go."

He lightly nudges my left shoulder, turning me around. Reluctantly, I followed. He tried to make small talk, but I kept my head down, my answers clipped.

"I'm Officer Donovan, Jacob Donovan. What is your name?" He had asked, looking over to me.

He continues as another one of his questions goes unanswered. "Now how are you going to have me give my full government and not give me yours?"

I couldn't help but laugh at this white man trying to talk slang. "What's so funny?" He smiles, holding his hands up in the air; knowing he was breaking down my walls.

"You're funny. You didn't give me your full government, what's your middle name?"

"Oh man! You want my middle name too? I don't think I've ever told anybody my middle name before, but I guess you're alright." He playfully bumps me. "It's Elmer. Jacob Elmer Donovan."

"Elmer!" I cried with laughter that halted my step. "Alright. Alright. You win Elmer, my name is Mikayla Collins, but everyone calls me Mickey."

"Win? Were we playing a game?" He laughs along with me, not at all offended. "Mickey, huh?"

"Yeah, that's me."

"Tell me Mickey, why are you out this time of night? Don't you have school in the morning?"

"Why do you care?" I asked, crossing my arms over my chest.

He shrugged. "Because someone should. Streets like these? I know them better than you'd think." He smiled faintly. "I know what it's like to feel like no one's watching your back."

His words threw me off guard, but I didn't want to admit it. Instead, I muttered, "I can handle myself and I'll get up. I never miss a day of school." I said boldly, and that wasn't a lie, I truly enjoyed school; not only because it was a temporary escape from my life.

"I'm sure you can," he said, genuine. "But you don't have to. Not tonight." He continued as we resumed our walk.

"What school you go to, Saint Mark the Evangelist?" I'm hit with yet another inquiry.

"Yup." I was getting tired of all the questions.

"So…" He had started but ceased when he realized I had stopped walking.

The street was dark, and you could literally smell the poverty and drugs in the air. It was still and dreary.

"You okay? Let's go."

With another nudge we journeyed down my street in silence. "I got it from here." I stated, as we approached my apartment building, putting my hand up to prevent him from coming up.

"I'm walking you to your door Mickey. Does your mother even know you're out at three in the morning?" He asked, his tone firm as he opens the entry door.

"This is me; 341." I stammer, head hanging low from the weight of anxiety and shame.

Before I could stop him, he knocked on the door. My heart sank. The man who answered was naked, his greasy skin glistening in the faint light of the hallway. Behind him, I saw my mother sprawled on the couch, a needle still dangling from her arm. The air was thick with the smell of sweat and regret.

I shoved past them both and locked myself in my room, trembling with a mix of fury and shame. By the time morning came, it was as if nothing had happened. Love didn't even notice I'd been gone.

I went to school like I always did, clutching the routine like a lifeline. But when the day ended, Officer Donovan and child protective services were waiting for me outside the gates. And now, here I was, waiting for a man who called himself my father.

"Aight, I'm here. Where she at? I got shit to do!" his deep voice boomed, full of impatience; dragging me back to now. I look up as a tall man storm past, his face expressionless.

My father. Apparently.

1

The sharp clang of a metal door echoed down the hallway, jolting me awake. My head snapped up, the sudden movement sending a dull ache rippling through my temples. Blinking against the harsh fluorescent light, I tried to focus. My surroundings blurred into sharp relief—a narrow cell, cold steel walls, and a smell so clinical it bordered on suffocating. This wasn't a nightmare. I was still here. Jail.

"Collins." barked a voice from somewhere outside the bars.

For a moment, I had been lost in the past, reliving a life I thought I had left behind. But there was no escaping now. I sat up slowly, every muscle in my body protesting. My Halston Heritage gown, once pristine and elegant, was now a crumpled mess that clung to my skin in all the wrong places. A quick glance in the small, scratched mirror bolted to the wall confirmed what I already suspected; I looked like hell. Mascara streaked like war paint down my cheeks, hair that had once been a crown now hung limp and knotted. A groan escaped me as I rubbed the stiffness from my neck.

"Collins!" The voice was closer this time, sharp and impatient.

"Alright, alright, I'm coming," I muttered, swinging my legs over the edge of the cot. The chill of the concrete floor seeped through the thin soles of my heels, making me wince. As I stood, the sound of jingling keys drew my attention to the officer unlocking my cell.

He was tall, broad, and had the kind of face that screamed, Don't try me. His uniform was crisp, his boots polished to a shine that caught the light.

"Let's go," he said, jerking his head toward the hallway.

"Nice to see you too," I shot back, my voice dripping with sarcasm. My humor felt brittle, like armor that wouldn't hold up under real pressure. Still, it was all I had.

He ignored me, stepping aside to let me pass. I adjusted my gown as best I could and walked out, chin high. The heels of my shoes clicked against the linoleum, the sound echoing in the narrow corridor. The fluorescent lights buzzed overhead, their sterile glow casting everything in a sickly yellow hue.

The officer's grip on my arm was firm but not rough as he led me past rows of identical cells. The air was thick with the scent of bleach and stale sweat, punctuated by the occasional murmur of voices or the metallic clang of distant doors. My mind raced, flipping through every memory of the last twenty-four hours, searching for an answer to the question I couldn't shake: How the hell did I end up here?

Raul's face flickered in my mind. His easy smile, his smooth words, the way he always made me feel like the world was ours for the taking. My stomach twisted. Where was he? Why wasn't he here, fighting to get me out of this mess?

The officer stopped in front of a plain metal door, pulling me out of my thoughts. He unlocked it with a loud click and gestured for me to enter. Inside, the room was small and windowless, its walls painted an uninspiring gray. A single bulb hung from the ceiling, casting harsh shadows on the steel table and chairs bolted to the floor. The air was colder here, as if the room itself fed off tension.

"Take a seat," he said, his tone leaving no room for argument. He guided me to the chair and snapped a cuff around my wrist, chaining me to the armrest.

"Wow," I said, raising my free hand in mock surrender. "All this for little ol' me? I feel special."

He didn't respond, just stepped back and left the room, the door slamming shut behind him. The sound was like a gunshot in the stillness, making me flinch. My heartbeat thundered in my ears, a steady drumbeat of rising anxiety. I forced myself to breathe, to focus on the table in front of me. Its surface was scratched and pitted, a silent witness to who-knew-how-many interrogations.

I didn't have to wait long. The door creaked open again, and a woman in a navy pantsuit stepped inside. Her polished shoes clicked against the floor, and she carried a file folder and notepad with the precision of someone who always knew where things belonged. Her hair was pulled back into a bun so tight it looked painful, and her expression was unreadable.

"Miss Collins," she began, setting the folder down with a soft thud. Her tone was calm but edged with authority. "I'm Sharon Cochran, lead investigator on your case."

"Case?" I repeated, my voice flat as I leaned back in the chair. "I don't have a case. I'm a legitimate business owner and a pillar of my community."

Cochran raised an eyebrow, unimpressed. "That may be true, but the evidence suggests otherwise."

"Evidence?" I shot back, my voice rising. "What evidence? Raul did this! Not me."

She didn't react to my outburst, instead opening the file in front of her. "I'll be asking the questions, Miss Collins."

I leaned forward, narrowing my eyes. "Am I being charged?"

"No," she said evenly. "Not yet."

"Then un-cuff me," I demanded, shaking the chained wrist for emphasis.

Cochran sighed, pulling a key from her pocket. She leaned over and unlocked the cuff. I rubbed my wrist, the red indentations a physical reminder of how far I'd fallen.

She slid a photograph across the table. "Do you recognize this man?" she asked, her voice sharpening.

"Yes," I said slowly. "That's Raul."

"Raul," she repeated, leaning back slightly. "Also known as Jason Montgomery."

The name hit me like a slap. I stared at her, waiting for the punchline. When it didn't come, I snorted. "Jason? No, you've got the wrong guy."

Her gaze didn't waver as she slid another photo across the table, followed by another. Each one showed Raul—or Jason—with different people in different places. The connections were clear, even if I didn't want to admit it.

"Or is it John Stevens? Maybe Mark Ruiz?" She began. "How about-"

"Am I being charged?" I asked again, pushing the photos back toward her. My voice was sharper now, a blade meant to cut through her questions. "Because if I am, I'd like to see my lawyer."

Cochran didn't flinch. "We're not here to charge you, Miss Collins. We're here to understand your involvement—or lack thereof."

"My lack thereof," I shot, leaning forward. "Whatever Raul did, it has nothing to do with me."

She tilted her head, studying me. "You trusted him, didn't you?" she asked, her voice softening just enough to sound like sympathy.

I clenched my jaw, refusing to let her see the cracks forming.

Cochran sighed, closing the file. "Miss Collins, Jason Montgomery has been conning people for years. If we don't stop him now, he won't just disappear—he'll ruin more lives. If you know anything—"

"I don't," I interrupted, my voice cracking slightly. "I don't know anything."

The words hung in the air, heavy and unconvincing. My chest tightened as the weight of the situation pressed down on me. Victim. That's what she was implying, wasn't it? That I was just another pawn in Jason's game. The thought made my stomach churn.

I stood abruptly, causing the table to scrap against the floor. "If I'm not being charged, we're done here."

Cochran didn't stop me. Instead, she leaned back in her chair, her hands folded neatly on the table. "You're free to leave, Miss Collins. But if you want to make this right—if you want to protect what's left of your reputation—you know where to find me."

I didn't respond. My heels clicked against the floor as I left the room, each step echoing in the hallway like a countdown. My thoughts churned, a storm of anger and betrayal that threatened to consume me. But one thing was clear: I wasn't going to let Jason—or anyone else—destroy what I'd built.

Not without a fight.

2

By the time I stepped outside the precinct, the midday sun was glaring down like a spotlight, exposing every crack in my carefully curated life. My phone buzzed incessantly in my bag—a mix of reporters, employees, and people I didn't recognize—but I couldn't deal with them. Not yet. Right now, I needed answers. Real answers. And I knew there was one person I could trust to help me find them. Bennett.

I slumped into the driver's seat of my car, gripping the wheel tightly as if it might steady the storm brewing inside me. My breath hitched, sharp and uneven. Everything felt too loud—the honk of distant car horns, the faint murmur of people walking by, even the sound of my own heartbeat hammering in my chest.

Fumbling for my phone, I scrolled through my contacts, each name blurring into the next until I landed on the one I needed. With a deep breath, I hit dial.

"Bennett & Associates, this is Chloe speaking. How may I assist you?"

"Chloe, it's Mickey Collins. I need to speak with Bennett. It's urgent."

There was a brief pause. "Of course, Ms. Collins. One moment."

The hold music played for only a few seconds before Bennett's deep, familiar voice came through the line.

"Mickey, to what do I owe the pleasure?" His tone was light, but I could hear the curiosity behind it.

"Cut the pleasantries, Bennett. I need you to pull everything you've got on my accounts. Every transaction, every loan, every investment. I want to know if anything's missing or… added."

"Added?" His voice sharpened. "What exactly are you looking for?"

I leaned my head back against the car seat, closing my eyes. "I'm not sure yet. Just… check everything. I've been distracted these last few months, and now I'm realizing that might have been a mistake. I need to know if Raul… or whoever he is… left me any surprises."

There was a pause. "Raul? The boyfriend?"

"Ex," I corrected sharply. "And yes, him. He's not who I thought he was. Turns out I was shacked up with a con artist. So, do what you do best and figure out if he's stolen from me or planted anything in my name."

Bennett's tone softened slightly. "I'll get on it right away. Are you sure you're okay?"

I let out a bitter laugh. "No, I'm not okay, Bennett. But I will be. Just call me as soon as you have something."

"You got it."

I ended the call, tossing my phone onto the passenger seat and gripping the wheel again. The tension in my chest was relentless, but I couldn't afford to dwell on it. I had to keep moving.

By 10 a.m., I was slipping through the back door of my boutique, avoiding the front entrance like a criminal ducking the spotlight. The store was buzzing with life—Monique managing the floor like a pro, Tesha laughing with customers in her hideous pink wig. New arrivals gleamed under the track lighting, and the cash register chimed as purchases rolled in.

It was a comforting scene, one I'd built from the ground up. But today, it felt fragile, as if one wrong move would send the whole operation crumbling.

I motioned to Monique as I passed, my voice low. "When you're done, meet me in my office."

She nodded, her usual efficiency unshaken by the undercurrent of tension in my tone.

In my office, I sank into my chair and pulled up the financials on my computer. The numbers stared back at me, each line item mocking my growing paranoia. I combed through every transaction, every vendor payment, every receipt, searching for something—anything—that didn't add up. But everything looked normal. Frustratingly, maddeningly normal.

A soft knock interrupted my spiraling thoughts. "Come in," I called, rubbing my temples.

Monique entered, her expression cautious. She closed the

door behind her and stood, waiting for my direction.

"Have a seat," I said, motioning to the chair across from me. "Listen, I'll get straight to it. I need you to hold down the fort for a while. Both here and Miami. Think you can handle it?"

Her eyes widened briefly before she straightened her back, pride flashing in her expression. "Of course, Ms. Collins. I'd be honored." Then her tone shifts. "Is everything okay? I mean, I've seen the news, and—"

My gaze hardened. "Mind your damn business, Monique. I asked you one simple question." I snapped, my voice cutting through the air like a whip. "All you need to know is that I'll be out of town, and you're in charge until I'm back. That clear?"

Her shoulders stiffened, but she nodded. "Yes, ma'am."

"Good." I stood, grabbing my purse and overcoat. I walked to the door, then paused, glancing back at her. "Oh, and Mo'?"

"Yes, Ms. Collins?"

"Fire Tesha."

Monique blinked, clearly startled. "Fire her? For what?"

"Because I said so." Her disturbed expression brought a faint smile to my face. "Heavy is the head that wears the crown."

Back in my car, I checked my watch. I had just enough time to pack before heading to the airport. The plan was simple: get to New York, find Raul, and make him pay. But as much as I wanted revenge, the closer I got to enacting it, the heavier the fear settled in my chest.

New York wasn't just a city to me—it was the life I had fought to leave behind. The hustle, the streets, the ghosts of who

I used to be. I'd spent years building something new, something better, and now I was heading straight back to the place where it had all started to unravel.

The ghosts waited for me there. The ones I'd walked away from without a second thought. The ones I'd hurt. The ones who'd hurt me. I could feel them already, their judgments like whispers in the wind. What if they still held grudges? Worse, what if they didn't? What if they let me back in, only to tear me apart again?

I gripped the steering wheel tighter, my breath coming in shallow bursts. The fear didn't make sense—I was Mickey Collins, for God's sake. I'd built an empire, walked through fire, and come out stronger. But here I was, terrified of facing ghosts I'd thought I'd buried.

I shook the thoughts away and started the engine. I'd face the ghosts when I got there. For now, all that mattered was getting to the airport.

3

Stepping onto the Hawker 900XP, I collapse into a window seat, tossing my bag onto the table in front of me. The sigh that escapes feels like it's been clawing at my chest all morning, waiting for release. The jet hums beneath my feet, a faint vibration that echoes the chaos in my head.

The pulse of the plane's engines fades into silence as my phone buzzes on the table in front of me. The screen flashes Bennett. My chest tightens.

I grab the phone, bracing myself. "Bennett."

"I've got the preliminary report," he says, skipping the pleasantries. His tone is clipped, serious. My pulse quickens.

"And?"

"It's bad, Mickey." Papers shuffle in the background, the sound sharp and unforgiving. "He didn't just steal from you. He used your accounts to launder money—hundreds of thousands—through shell companies."

The words don't register immediately. "What are you talking about? My accounts are clean."

"Not anymore," Bennett replies grimly. "Raul—Jason, or

whatever alias he's using this week—left a paper trail so messy it's a miracle the feds aren't back at your door already."

The air in the cabin feels suddenly thinner. "You're telling me he not only stole from me but made me a criminal?"

"Yes," Bennett says, his voice softening slightly. "And Mickey... it's worse than that. He forged your signature on multiple offshore accounts. This isn't just theft. It's deliberate."

Deliberate. The word lands like a punch, knocking the air from my lungs. My fingers tighten around the phone until it feels like it might snap.

"That son of a bitch wanted to destroy me," I hiss, the rage bubbling beneath my skin. "This wasn't just about money."

"No," Bennett says. "It wasn't. He wanted to burn everything you've built to the ground."

I don't respond, the silence between us heavy and charged. Finally, Bennett clears his throat. "Mickey, you need to act fast. The longer this goes unchecked—"

"I know," I snap, cutting him off. "Just... do your job, Bennett."

I hang up before he can say another word, tossing the phone onto the table. My hands are shaking, my nails digging into my palms hard enough to leave marks. Jason wanted to destroy me. Fine. But he forgot one thing: I've been built to survive worse than him.

I stare out the oval window, watching the ground crew shuffle about, their movements purposeful, unlike my own, fire now simmering inside of me. My carefully crafted world is unraveling thread by thread, and I'm struggling to hold the ends.

I close my eyes, letting the dull thrum of the engines pull me away. But memories are like smoke—they seep into the smallest cracks.

Harlem, 1999

The first time I met Hakeem Collins—my father—I learned what power looked like up close. The streets called him "Stone." To me, he was a stranger with my face.

Stone was Harlem's king, a title he wore like armor. Drugs, guns, women—he controlled them all. Everyone either wanted to be him or be with him. But for all his bravado, it was his mixed heritage that set him apart. With his honey-colored skin and wavy hair, he looked more Puerto Rican than Black, but his deep, commanding voice left no doubt about his roots.

The first time I laid eyes on him, I knew. This man was why I looked the way I did, why my mom never spoke of him. He stood tall—at least six feet—dressed like royalty in navy slacks and a pale blue shirt. A thick gold pinky ring glinted in the sunlight, a little flashy for my taste, but then again, I wasn't the one ruling Harlem.

"Now, listen up," he said, once I was in his car, clutching my duffel bag like a life raft. "You're gonna hear a lot about me. Believe all of it."

His voice rose slightly, commanding my attention. "This is my city. You understand? And since it's my city, it's yours too. I know your mom's been... going through it, but while you're with me, you don't have to worry about a thing."

His stern face softened, just for a moment, and he smiled—a smile that felt almost safe. But as quickly as it came, it vanished.

"As long as you do what I say."

I hugged my bag tighter and nodded, too scared to speak. For a split second, I thought life might return to some kind of normal. His next move shattered that illusion. Reaching for the stereo, he cranked it to full blast, and Jay-Z's "So Ghetto" filled the car.

As we drove deeper into Harlem, the streets came alive. Kids played stickball, hustlers leaned against cars, and music from a dozen different boom boxes filled the air. The convertible top came down, and suddenly, Q-Tip's "Vivrant Thing" was our soundtrack. If you'd told me this moment would spark my love for hip-hop, I wouldn't have believed you.

"Hakeem! Hakeem!" Voices rang out as we crawled down 123rd Street. A woman in cut-off denim shorts and a rainbow-striped halter top sauntered in front of the car, forcing us to stop. Her lips smacked as she stared him down.

"You don't know nobody now?" she spat, leaning against the driver's side door.

Stone didn't flinch. She whispered something in his ear, her nails tapping on the window frame. Whatever she said, it didn't faze him.

"Word." That was his only response before pulling away, leaving her standing in the street.

We crossed borough lines into Brooklyn, where the vibe was

the same: project buildings, hustlers, and kids in the streets.

"Aye, yo Stone! Hold up!" A young dude yells out, exiting a corner store.

He hopped in the backseat without hesitation. "What up, Book?" Hakeem daps him up.

"Ride me over to Bank block. That nigga just seeing me with you will make him come off what's owed to ya boy. I won't even flash my piece." Book adjusts himself in the seat, pulling out his gun and laying it on his thigh, then finally noticing me.

"Yo, who the shorty? This ya new lady?"

"That's my seed nigga."

"My bad, I ain't know. She mad cute though." He cuts his eyes over to me and grins.

"Watch your mouth little homie, don't let me have to shoot you in front of my daughter on her first day with me."

"Naw, you got it boss." Book put his hands up as if in surrender, then pulling his oversized t-shirt over his gun as though he was hiding it.

"This Mickey, she gonna be with me for a little while."

"What up Mickey, I'm Booker but everybody call me Book." He reaches his hand over the seat to shake mine.

"Hey." Is the only thing I say. I didn't even shake his hand. I'm not the quiet type, never have been, but this was observation time. It was not the time for pleasantries. He had pulled his hand away after realizing I would not give him mine. I never looked at him, but I could feel his eyes burning into the side of my face.

"There go that fat ass nigga Stone." Booker's attention is taken away as we come up on the Van Dyke projects. Book jumps out the car. Hakeem stops the car and puts it in park. He steps out and leans against it, smoothing out his attire, then folding his arms across his chest. "Don't move." He looks back at me with a look so cold, I got chills.

"Yo Bank, where my money homie?" Booker yells out, making his way to the man that owed him. Bank seemed frightened when he notices Hakeem across the street. He pays no attention to Book; loping past him and straight over to Stone.

"Hakeem, my man! You know how it get, but don't worry, I got your money fo sho." He was sweating and talking too fast. I knew he was lying, and I didn't even know him.

"I mean I got ya money, not all of it though." He continued, pulling a wad of one hundred dollar bills out of his pocket. "But I'll have the rest real soon. Real soon on god."

Without saying a word, Hakeem punches the shit out of Bank, who crumbles to the ground. He reaches down and picks up the money that had just fallen.

"You disappoint me Bankhead. You don't smoke the product." He finally speaks, adjusting his clustered gold pinky ring before pointing his finger down into Bank's face as though it was a gun. I had never seen a grown man so scared in my life.

"What? You thought I didn't know nigga? I know everything motherfucker. You done in these streets. I have given you too many chances, wanting all my brothers to eat, but you'll never make another dollar or smoke another rock. Next time I see you, I want all of mines, you hear me?" Hakeem kicks him in the stomach and gets back in the car, leaving him in the middle of the street, balled up in a fetal position.

"Book, find another way back." He yells out without turning around. He throws the tattered wad of money at me. "This yours now, buy yourself some clothes and shoes. Get your hair and toes done or what not." He tells me, keeping his eyes on the road.

"Say thank you." He demands.

"Thank you." I mumble, hating every word.

We continue our ride through the Bronx and then into Queens where the "King" played politician, shaking hands, kissed babies, and collected money. The sun began to go down and I knew we just had to be close to his house.

"Where are we going now?" At last, I had decided to open my mouth and speak. I had started really taking in my surroundings and it was looking like we were going into the city.

"Home."

"I thought home was back there."

He turns down the Mobb Deep that played and said, "Just because I run the hood, doesn't mean I want to live there. You never eat where you shit Mick, remember that."

The car slows as we turn into the driveway of the Upper Echelon apartment building. He drives up to the main entrance, where a little white man runs out and opens my door.

"Welcome home Mr. Collins."

"Thank you, Stewart. This is my daughter Mickey. Her mother has suddenly fallen ill, so she will be staying with me for a while. I want you to make sure she is taken care of." Hakeem replies, handing the doorman a fifty-dollar bill and his keys.

"Yes sir Mr. Collins, absolutely."

As we walk in, I am taken aback by the beauty of the building. The inside was just as grand as the outside. Everyone was so nice and well put together; it made me uncomfortable and self-conscious. I begin to fix my appearance as we walked through the lobby.

We make it to the elevator and if I didn't realize how extravagant the place was when we arrived, I definitely realized it then. The elevator displayed fifteen floors and Hakeem puts his finger on the Penthouse button.

The elevator doors open to the apartment foyer, the floors were marble as far as the eye could see. Following him inside, he points out each room to me.

"Here's the kitchen, living room, guest bath, game area, your room is down there to the left, my room is on the other side of the house. Make yourself at home."

With that he left me standing there and went toward his room. Once I heard a door shut, I dropped my bag and stood there for what seemed and probably was hours.

This was my new reality.

4

I'm jolted awake by loud noises. Morning. I didn't even realize I'd fallen asleep on the couch. Lifting my head, I spot Hakeem in the kitchen, cooking.

"I know you know you have a room, right? You know how I know? Because I told you where it is last night."

"I know, I must've been exhausted." I mumble, sitting up and dragging myself to one of the stools by the island.

"Breakfast is the most important part of the day." He slides a plate of scrambled eggs in front of me. "Here. Eat."

He grabs toast from the counter and adds it to my plate. "I'm heading out. Oh, and this"—he pulls a Nokia from his pocket—"is your new phone. My number's already in it. Only call me if someone's trying to kill you, and don't lose it."

"Yes sir." I glance at the phone, excitement bubbling up. I had never had anything like it. "Thank you." I look up at him with a smile and I noticed his face had become softer.

"Your cousin Bird's coming over. You two are about the same age. Maybe go shopping or something."

Hakeem pulls out two thick stacks of cash from his other

pocket. The bills look brand new, unlike the crumpled mess from yesterday. Each stack is wrapped with $10,000 written on it.

"This should be enough," he continues. "When you get back, Thomas is expecting you at 5 o'clock to take your fingerprint. You'll need it to get back in. Don't..."

He stops mid-sentence as his phone rings. "Yeah." He answers, heading for the elevator. And like that, he is gone, and I am yet again – alone.

I look down at the plate in front of me and push it aside. Standing up, I take in space; the bathroom's to my left. I grab my bag and head in to freshen up. The room's spotless—no leaks, no grime. The mirror's clear. I see myself: hair a mess, bags under my eyes, clothes dingy. I look as bad as that social worker.

Forget it. No longer wanting to look at myself, I flip the light off and throw my bag across my shoulder. I already feel out of place, might as well be noisy. Maybe my so-called dad's room has something worth looking at.

But as soon as I try to open the door, it starts beeping, a blue light flashing on the handle. Right. Fingerprint. I press my thumb against it. It turns red and beeps louder. Instinct has me running, and by the time it stops, I'm across the apartment, in my new room.

The only thing different from this room and all the others, is that there was a pop of color in the all-white apartment, and that came from grey headboard on the low standing queen bed. It's nothing special; it was not made to be welcoming or designed for a teenager. It's not full of color and sweet smells. There are no girlie items or filled with the things that interest me. But what could I possibly expect? This man did not know me. Even though I could tell there is a soft area in him, this man does not care about me. Throwing money at me and ghosting, he was no better than my mama.

I toss my bag onto the bed and collapse beside it, staring at the ceiling. So much has happened in the last 48 hours, and I still can't wrap my head around it. But just as I start to think, a phone rings.

I look around and realize it's not the Nokia Hakeem had gave me. It's coming from the kitchen. A cordless phone on the end table in the living room is ringing. I answer it hesitantly.

"Hello."

"Good Morning Ms. Collins, this is Thomas from the front desk. I have a Tamika Mathers here; shall I send her up?"

Tamika? Must be Bird, my cousin. "Yes."

"Certainly. Thank you, ma'am."

I smile at how polite he is as I hang up. Running back to my room, I grab my bag and head for the bathroom to change and brush my teeth.

And then, I see it.

Is this my bathroom? A glass shower and a clawfoot tub, the kind you only see in magazines. A vanity full of toiletries. I can't believe this is real.

"Hey girl."

I spin around, startled. Bird's here. She's slim, almond brown skin, long hair, and those big, round light eyes. We definitely share blood.

"Uh, hey." I blink, thrown off guard.

"You can't be serious." She scans me up and down. "What are you wearing?"

"Clothes," I reply flatly, hand on my hip. I'm still in yesterday's flannel and bell bottoms, but I'm owning it.

"Don't get testy, cousin. That ain't clothes. You're in dire need. Come here." She motions me into the room.

Flinging open the doors to the closet, stepping back like she's showing me a treasure chest.. "These are clothes babygirl."

The closet is packed with designer everything—clothes, handbags. What's the point of shopping if I've got all this? Bird digs through the racks for a while, then steps back, triumphant.

"Girl, it's 1999. You can't be out here looking like this. Not with me, and especially not as Hakeem Collins's daughter. You're royalty now." She says the last part like it's a curse.

She flings a pair of Tommy Hilfiger short overalls and a matching tube top on the bed, then hands me a pair of Sean Witherspoon Nike Air Max. "Put this on." And with that, she leaves me to change.

I haven't felt so exposed in my life wearing this outfit. I walk out feeling uncomfortable in my skin.

"Now that's what I'm talking about!" Bird gets up from the sofa, turning off the TV. "Now you can be seen with your girl. And you got a banging little body too." She shakes her head as in agreement with herself and smiles. "Grab your money and purse and let's go."

"I don't have a purse."

Bird rolls her eyes, disappears into my room, and returns with a small black Coach crossbody.

"Here," she hands it to me, examining me more closely. She reaches up, touches my hair, then smiles. "Alright, I know our first stop. Let's go."

5

"Thank you, Kitty!" I shout as we step out of Crown Me Hair Salon in Queens. My blowout and silkening have my hair laid like a crown, glistening under the sunlight. When I catch a glance of myself in the floor-to-ceiling mirror, it's almost like I'm staring at a stranger. My reflection stares back at me—an image of power, confidence, someone who belongs. I'm a far cry from the girl I was just a day ago.

"Damn, what I tell you?" Bird's voice cuts through my thoughts as she steps up behind me, grinning ear to ear. "Kitty's a wizard with them hands. You lookin' like a queen."

"You weren't lying," I say, running my fingers through my smooth, silky hair. It feels different. I feel different. Something about this new look is starting to settle into my skin, like the first time I wore makeup or put on a new outfit that made me feel like I could conquer the world.

But I know better than to get too comfortable. Confidence is one thing. Trusting this feeling is another. I've learned the hard way that when everything seems too perfect, it usually means something's off. Gotta stay sharp, gotta stay ready. I need to stay on my toes, because if I slip, no telling where else I might end up.

Bird laughs, tugging at my arm to pull me out of the door. "C'mon, girl. You're looking too good to be standing here all day."

"So, what's next?" I ask, trying to keep my mind on track as she drags me down the street.

"You hungry?" she asks with a raised brow.

"I could eat," I say, my stomach growling loud enough to answer for me. I should've eaten those eggs earlier.

"Alright, we headed to Mama's," Bird says casually.

"To your mama's?"

"Nah, girl. Betty's down the block. She Travis' mama—cooks for the whole neighborhood. Ya daddy offered to buy her a little restaurant once, but she told him she likes keeping it in her tiny apartment. Her food's fire though," Bird shrugs, like it's the most normal thing in the world. "Plus, this'll be your chance to meet some folks. From Queens to the Bronx, you need to know who's who around here."

"Ugh, I'm not ready to meet a bunch of new people, Bird," I groan. "Can't we just hit a diner or something?"

"Girl you the daughter of…"

"Hakeem Collins. Yeah, you've said that already." I'm agitated.

"You damn right, and don't you forget it!" She laughs, raising her hands in amused disbelief. "You a queen out here in these streets, you need to meet your subjects."

She has really lost her mind. If Hakeem Collins is all that, where the hell has he been all these years. I don't feel like royalty. Right now, I feel like I'm getting dragged into a life I never asked for.

"Girl, I don't know that man!" I'm going to have to break it down for her. "Everything you talkin' about right now, doesn't mean shit to me. It sure as hell would have been nice to be royalty years ago. I don't know him, and he doesn't know me, and I can tell you right now, neither one of us want that shit to change."

I could tell I surprised her with my outpour of resentment; she stops walking as we were about to walk into the building. "Listen, I know how you feeling right now Mickey." She gets serious with me. "Our family was dealt a bad hand. Ya moms a crackhead and mine's doing life on Rikers Island. I know Unc ain't been there for you, I don't know nothing about all that, but at least yo ass got a daddy - mine died before I was even born. If it wasn't for Unc being who he is, I wouldn't have made it out here. And you won't make it in this life either if you don't understand and accept who you are. You a boss, you hear me?" She grabs my face and stares at me intensely until I answer.

"I guess." I mutter, unsure but willing to let her words settle for now.

6

As soon as we step inside Betty's apartment, a thick cloud of smoke hits me—half fried chicken, half blunts. It's an aroma that immediately tells me this is no place for the faint of heart.

"Damn, somebody crack a window!" Bird yells, waving her hand in front of her face like the smoke is a personal attack.

"Yo, what's good 'B'?" A tall, lanky, dark-skinned dude gets up from the couch to hug my cousin. "You heard her nigga; open the damn window. Let some of this smoke out in this bitch." He instructs the guy in a chair by the window. His eyes quickly flick to me, scanning me from head to toe like he's figuring me out in one second.

"Mick, this is Roger." Bird introduces me, pulling away from their hug. "Roger, this my cousin Mickey; Stone's daughter."

His eyes widen, then a devious grin takes over. "Wait. Word?" His whole demeanor shifts, turning from surprised to calculating. He grabs my hand a little too hard, pulling me closer like we've known each other for years. "Yo! This Mickey, Stone's little girl!" he shouts to the room, as if the name is supposed to mean something to everyone.

The room falls quiet for a moment, then a few heads nod, a few people wave, but mostly, everyone's eyeing me. I'm not sure if it's because of who my dad is or just because I'm the new girl in the room.

"Mickey, this my crew." Roger points around the room. "We run East Harlem. That's E-Man, Forty, Big Sal, Marco, and his girl Diamond. Make sure you tell your pops we looked out for you and held you down."

I barely acknowledge them. What am I supposed to say? Yeah, I'm supposed to be some kind of royalty, but all I feel right now is exposed. Like I'm walking into a world that's about to chew me up and spit me out if I don't figure out how to play the game.

"Where mama at?" Bird asks Roger.

"In the kitchen with Trav." Roger responds, nodding toward the back.

Bird nudges me, leading me through the haze of smoke and bodies, the entire time I'm being observed and being observant until we hit the kitchen.

"Hey Birdy." Bird is greeted as soon as we cross over the kitchen threshold.

Mama is a hefty woman. You could tell she had been through a lot in her days, but her energy was welcoming. A smile and sense of comfort comes over me as I watch her; how she embraces Bird in a hug and plants a kiss on her cheek like she's the only one in the world. I can tell its genuine, and now I'm pretty sure she feels the same way about all the young people in her house.

"How are you baby?" She asks.

"I'm good." Bird responds. "I wanted to introduce you to my cousin." She turns to me, wrapping her arm around Mama's waist. "Mama, this is Mickey, my Uncle Hakeem's daughter."

"Oh well hey there baby! I should have known, you standin' over there looking just like him." She chuckles, coming over for a hug, arms wide open.

"It's nice to meet you." I step in for the embrace.

"Well, aren't you well spoken." She pulls back and uses both of her hands to grab my face. "You hungry?" Asking cheerfully.

"Yes ma'am."

"Hell Yeah." Bird adds in, practically licking her lips.

Laughing, Betty responds. "The food will be done in just a minute. You two make yourselves at home. Travis you and Booker get up from them there chairs and let these young ladies sit down." She waves us toward the table.

I didn't realize the boy from yesterday was sitting at the table in the dining room until I look over and my eyes run into his. There he was—Booker, with a lingering grin, and next to him, Travis. They were hunched over, their fingers quick and practiced as they weighed out bags of weed on a scale.

"Yo what's up shorty?" Booker holds his head up and smirks as if he is genuinely happy to see me.

"Hey." I mumble back, walking slowly toward them as Bird led the way.

KITTEN HEELS

She didn't hesitate—just walked right over to Travis and plopped herself in his lap like she belonged there. She wrapped her arm around his shoulder, the way couples do when they've got a little something going on. It was so casual, too natural for me to ignore.

"So y'all already know each other?" Bird asked, turning between Booker and me with a teasing smile, not a care in the world.

"Oh yeah, I met shorty yesterday when 'Keem rolled through the hood," Booker answered, his tone almost smug.

"You still acting stank today?" He added with the gum he was chewing showing through the side of his mouth.

I couldn't help but notice how good he looked. The Polo Sport hoodie, the crisp white Adidas, his low-cut hair edged just right—it all came together effortlessly. His teeth were white and straight, the kind that made girls stop and stare. He was everything that I usually wouldn't go for, but in this moment, I couldn't help but feel a little caught off guard. Still, I wasn't the type to let myself get pulled into someone's game so easily.

I ignored his question, turning my attention, hoping he'd take the hint. But of course, Bird wasn't about to let it slide.

"That's why I wanted to holla at you and Trav," she said, glancing back and forth between Booker and me. "See if y'all wanna help me show her around."

"Oh fo sho, no doubt," Travis piped in, his voice full of certainty as he zipped up the last bag of weed. He gave Bird a playful squeeze on the thigh. "But hold up, let me talk to you for a minute," he added, standing up and pulling her with him down the quiet hallway behind us.

I blinked, trying to process what had just happened. Bird, without so much as a second glance, walked off with Travis, leaving me here, completely alone in a room full of people I barely knew.

My arms crossed over my chest involuntarily, the irritation bubbling up. "Seriously?" I say in a low tone, my gaze following them as they disappeared down the hallway.

Booker noticed me standing there, arms folded like I was ready to throw a tantrum. "Well, you gonna sit down?" he asked, his voice light, teasing, like he was genuinely trying to draw me back into the conversation.

I glared at the hallway, seeing that Bird wasn't coming back anytime soon. So, I reluctantly plopped down into the seat where Travis had just been. I pushed the scale and the neatly bagged product aside, making room for myself as if I could ignore the reality of what was happening.

Booker stood up, gathering the bags and the scale into a bookbag with a quickness that almost made it look rehearsed. He was definitely used to this. "Does this kinda thing bother you?" He looked at me, his tone a little more curious than I expected.

I glanced at the products, the white bags filled with something illegal, something I could smell even if I couldn't see it clearly. "No," I said, my voice flat. "Just don't want it in my

KITTEN HEELS

face." I paused for a moment, then added, "How ya'll just gonna do this kind of stuff out in the open like that anyway? She don't mind?" I pointed toward Betty, who was at the counter, cooking up a storm.

"Who? Ma Dukes?" Booker chuckled, clearly amused by my question. "Oh nah, she don't mind. She figures Travis is gonna do it anyway, might as well keep an eye on him. On all of us, actually," he explained, tossing the bookbag over his shoulder as if it was just another part of his day. "Plus, we do all the big money shit somewhere else," he whispered, giving me a devious wink.

I raised an eyebrow. "Big money shit?" I repeated, surprised by his frankness.

Booker only shrugged, as though that part of the conversation was already over. He straightened up, the casual air returning to his demeanor. "Anyway, look," he said, his voice shifting back to the nonchalant tone from before, "I'm about to run downstairs to the corner store. Wanna roll?"

It was tempting, honestly. I didn't know when Bird would be back, and sitting alone in this house, surrounded by people who seemed to have their own agenda, didn't sound like fun. Plus, the food smelled like it was finally close to being ready, but it would probably be a while before anything actually hit the table.

"I'm hungry, though," I said, eyeing the kitchen. "Isn't the food almost done?"

"Come on, I got you," he said with an easy smile, his hand

motioning for me to get up and follow him. His confidence was undeniable, almost infectious.

I hesitated, taking in the way he stood there, waiting for me to make a decision. There was something about the way he looked at me, like he wasn't expecting me to say no, but he wasn't rushing me either. It made me feel like I had control in a situation where, frankly, I didn't feel like I had much.

I gave him one last hard look, weighing my options. His eyes didn't flinch, and neither did I. Finally, I sighed and stood up. "Alright, let's go."

He turned to Betty, already making his way toward the door. "Hey, Ma Dukes, we runnin' down to the store. You need me to pick something up?"

"Can you bring an old woman back a pint of milk and a ticket for the lotto?" she asked, her voice warm but still tinged with the edge of experience. It was a request that felt almost ritualistic, part of the dance that everyone seemed to play around here.

"Yeah, I got you, Ma," Booker said, laughing as he made his way toward the door, looking back at me. "Come on, shorty, we out."

"Guess my name's just gonna be 'shorty' now, huh?" I muttered under my breath, following him out into the street.

As we stepped outside, his pager went off. He paused for a moment, glancing at the number, then made his way over to a payphone. The booth was missing the door, and I couldn't hear what he was saying, but I noticed the way his posture shifted—

like he was handling something serious, like he was always handling something. He didn't even give me a second look as he made the call, like he was lost in his own world.

He didn't stay long, though. As soon as the conversation ended, he came back to me, all casual again. "Aight, shorty. So there's this Haitian spot down the block, and trust me, the food's banging. How's that sound?"

"Yeah, let's do it," I said, feeling my stomach rumble in agreement.

He clapped his hands together with a grin that was hard to resist. "Alright, cool," he said, already turning on his heel and taking the lead. "Follow me, shorty."

He wasted no time with small talk, but as we walked, he hit me with a question that caught me off guard.

"So... why you be acting all stank?"

I couldn't help but laugh, though the sound was short and sarcastic. "Ha! How have I been acting stank?"

He turned around to look at me, walking backward with a teasing glint in his eyes. "Man, I tried to introduce myself yesterday when you were with your pops, and you straight dogged me. Then today, you act like you don't even know ya boy."

I shrugged, not bothering to hide my indifference. "I don't."

He stopped walking for a second, his smile slipping just a little before he continued, "You know me enough to let me take you to get something to eat."

I paused, the words hitting me differently now. "Look," I

said, stopping in my tracks, "I can just go back and wait on Bird."

"Naw, naw," he said quickly, his tone shifting. "I'm just playing, hold up." He grabbed my hand, his grip light but firm. "It's all good, shorty. Just messing with you. You'll get to know me real well, don't worry." He shot me with a sly grin, and for some reason, I couldn't bring myself to pull away.

There was something about him—something that felt familiar, yet distant. Something in his eyes, the way he held himself, that made me wonder if this was exactly the kind of trouble I didn't need in my life. Still, I followed him, curiosity gnawing at me, even as I could feel the pull of something I couldn't quite define.

We weave through the crowded sidewalk, pushing through the warm, late-afternoon bustle until we reach the entrance of Nana's Bistro.

"Ayo, Derrick!" Booker calls out, his voice cutting through the crowd and noise, making the guy at the door glance up.

"What's good, 'B'?" Derrick responds, giving Booker a quick nod and clearing a path for us.

"Can we get a seat?" Booker asks, dapping him up.

"Oh, for sure. Follow me." Derrick says, leading us to the back where a cozy two-top by the window is waiting. The people he moved aside murmur under their breath, but we're already too far to hear them.

Derrick pulls out the chair for me, setting the mood with a casual "What you want?"

Booker jumps in before I can open my mouth. "Two jerk chickens with rice and peas, and some of that orange pop."

"Word," Derrick says, scribbling down the order before disappearing into the kitchen.

Before I could check Booker for having the nerve to order for me, his pager goes off again, pulling his attention.

"Excuse me, shorty. I'll be right back." He states before walking away.

I sink back in my seat, staring out the window, wishing for a bit of peace, but all the people between me and the world outside block my view.

When Derrick returns, he hands me a glass of the sweet orange pop. "Food's coming up, lil' mama," he adds, as if I'm impatient.

A woman soon follows, placing the fragrant plates in front of me. The spicy scent of jerk chicken hits my nose, and my stomach growls, reminding me how hungry I really am. It smelled too good. I know the polite thing to do is to wait for Booker to get back, but he knows what it is. I let it be known that I was hungry, so I don't think he would expect me to wait.

7

"Dang girl! You was hungry for real, huh?" Booker startles me as he comes back to the table. I had devoured my food.

"I told you." I respond with my mouth full, wiping my face with a napkin, now embarrassed.

"You wasn't lying." He laughs, sitting down.

"What took you so long?" I ask, changing the subject.

"Had to handle some business. Money never sleeps shorty."

"Okay, what's with all the 'shorty' talk?" I ask, raising an eyebrow. "You know that's not my name, right?"

"What? You don't like being called shorty?"

"No. I'm not a chickenhead. Call me Mickey or Mick; no more Shorty." I say, dropping my napkin on my plate, letting him know I was done.

He grins. "A'ight, no more 'shorty.' I got you, Mick." He shovels rice into his mouth, barely missing a beat. "Damn, you hard on a brother." He smacks. "That's good though, you need to keep that about yourself, you gonna need that in life."

I glance out the window, feeling the city pulse around

us. I've been hearing everyone talk about how I need to act, adapt, and survive. Like my life's been easy. It hasn't. I know the streets; Harlem's been teaching me all I need to know since birth.

"So, how long you been knowing Hakeem?" I ask, picking up my last chicken wing and biting it. Observation time was over, it's time to start asking questions.

"I been knowing your pops for a little minute now. We did a buck at Rikers together, been rocking ever since. He's taught me everything I know about the game, how to be a leader and a boss." He finishes with an expression of admiration across his face.

"At Rikers? How old are you?" He had a grown man air about him, but he didn't look old enough to be doing time in prison.

"Seventeen." He admits arrogantly, smiling from ear to ear.

"Well, how old were you when you did your bid?"

"Oh, yeah, I was fifteen."

"Fifteen?!" I almost spit my drink out at his response. "Shouldn't you have been in juvie? What did you do?"

"Yo, they don't care about all that around here shorty. If you black, young or old, you an adult in the court's eyes." He responds with a bothered sigh, tossing his fork down on his plate and sitting back in his chair.

"Me and my brother hit a couple homes back in the day, the judge tried us as adults and the rest is history; it is what it is." His voice had grown distant, and I notice the light in his eyes dims. It's clear this part of his past isn't something he likes revisiting.

The vibe gets awkwardly quiet, I don't know what to say. Should I hug him? Before I can even think of what to say or do, I feel a vibration in my seat. Looking around beside me, I realize that its' my purse that's vibrating. Opening it up, I see the ringing cell phone.

"Hello?" I answer the phone, trying to shake the awkward vibe.

"Where you at?" Hakeem's voice is sharp, laced with frustration.

"I'm at Nana's Bistro, grabbing a bite."

"Didn't I tell you that you needed to meet Thomas at five to get your shit in the system."

"Yes." I had forgotten all about getting my fingerprints taken.

"Then tell me why Thomas just called me, wanting to know if my daughter was still needing to get into the building?"

"I…"

"Na, don't even answer that. I got too many motherfuckers to look after and make sure they do what they supposed to be doing, I shouldn't have to do that with you, you should already know."

"I…"

"Look." He cuts me off again. "I told Thomas that if you not there in twenty minutes, then you not getting back in today. You'll have to figure out your own accommodations for tonight." With that the call was ended. As I stare at the phone in my hand, my skin is hot and I'm on the verge of tears.

I look up and catch Booker's eyes fixated on me.

"Ya man checking up on you?" He asks with a low laugh.

"Hakeem." I respond dryly, my mood souring. "Look, you know how to get in touch with Bird'em?"

Booker quickly digs out his phone and dials. "Ayo, Trav, put Bird on the line," he says. The phone's passed to me, and Bird's voice fills my ear.

"Yeah?"

"This Mickey. Hakeem's pissed, says I got twenty minutes to get my stuff in the system, or I'm out." My words spill out, rushed. It is already going to take me an hour and a half to get back by train. I could drop that time down to thirty minutes by taking Grand Central Parkway, but neither me nor Booker driving, and we would still be past the mark. I'm wasting time on this phone, and we haven't even paid for our food.

"Okay, I'll catch up with you tomorrow. You with Booker, right?"

"Yeah," I grumble.

"Good, he'll make sure you're straight." She pauses, but I don't respond. "Alright, I'll talk to you tomorrow, Mick."

The line goes dead.

8

"Yo, where you going?" Booker's voice called out, breathless and insistent as he jogged up to me. His face was flushed, but his dark eyes were sharp, scanning me like he could see all the emotions I was trying to bury.

I didn't stop. I couldn't. My feet moved faster, my chest tight with anger. "I gotta get back to the Upper East," I snapped, waving down a cab. My breath fogged in the cool air as I climbed in, slamming the door behind me. The stale stench of cigarette smoke hit me immediately, clinging to the fabric seats and pressing against my skin like a bad memory. I rolled down the window, letting the evening air cut through the haze.

Before I could tell the driver my destination, the door yanked open, and Booker slid in beside me. "Hold up, shorty," he said, still catching his breath. "You just gonna leave me like that?"

I shot him a glare. "You don't have to come with me."

"Yes, I do," he said firmly, his tone leaving no room for argument. "What kind of man would I be if I let you ride off by yourself across the city? Ain't no way you're making it there in twenty minutes. What you gone do?"

His words settled on me like a weight, the truth of them pressing into my chest. Hakeem didn't play. I'd known that when I'd stormed out, but now, sitting in the cab with Booker's steady gaze on me, the reality felt sharper.

"I don't know," I admitted finally, leaning back in the seat. My hands rested in my lap, my fingers twitching as if they could find an answer in the fabric of my jeans. I stared up at the car's stained ceiling, my vision blurring slightly as I locked onto a single spot.

Booker didn't push, but I could feel his presence beside me—solid and unshaken, like an anchor. My mind drifted, the soft hum of the taxi lulling me into a vision of a future I wasn't sure I believed in yet. It wasn't clear, just fragments of feelings: happiness, love, freedom. A version of me who wasn't carrying the weight of everyone else's mistakes.

I inhaled deeply, the cool air biting at my throat, and made a quiet decision. I wasn't a scared little girl anymore. I wasn't powerless, and I wasn't going to keep letting life happen to me. Hakeem, Bird, whoever—I had been taking care of myself for years anyway. This was just another step.

The cab slowed, and I glanced at my phone. The screen lit up with the time: 6:15 p.m. Too late. I exhaled sharply, my stomach tightening. Booker must have sensed it because his hand brushed against mine lightly. "You good, shorty?"

I pulled my hand away and opened my purse, grabbing a

crisp hundred-dollar bill. "I'm fine," I said quickly, handing the money to the driver. The door creaked as I stepped out, the sound grating against my nerves. Booker followed, his footsteps heavy behind me.

Before I could take another step, Thomas appeared, his expression pinched with concern. "Miss Collins," he started, his tone polite but firm.

I didn't need him to finish to know what was coming. "I'm too late, huh?" My voice was even, but I could feel the anger bubbling under my skin.

"I'm sorry, Miss Collins," he said, his hands clasped tightly in front of him. "Your father instructed me not to allow you in if you weren't here by five. He insisted it was for your own good—a lesson, he said."

A bitter laugh escaped me before I could stop it. Of course. Hakeem didn't just demand control—he thrived on it. I turned back to the cab, leaning into the open door. "Take me to Harlem."

"What's in Harlem?" Booker asked, his voice breaking through the tension. I had almost forgotten he was still there.

"Huh?" I blinked, caught off guard. "Oh…my girl Carmen." It was the only place I could think of where I might feel safe—welcomed.

Booker tilted his head, studying me. "Why you wanna go there?" he asked, his tone lighter now, almost teasing. "Don't let this shit ruin your night, shorty. We're in the city—let's enjoy it."

He tapped the driver's shoulder. "Take us to Times Square."

"What?!" I turned to him, my eyes narrowing. "Booker, I'm not in the mood—"

"Relax," he said, cutting me off with a grin. "I got you. Just trust me for once."

I stared at him, my walls instinctively going up. But his eyes held mine, steady and warm, and I felt my guard slip, just a little. Maybe he was right. Maybe I needed to let go for one night, to stop carrying the weight of everything I couldn't control.

"Fine," I said, leaning back against the seat. The cab pulled away, the city lights reflecting off the windows. Booker's grin widened, sending a faint jolt through me.

9

The cab finally pulled to a stop, its engine idling as Booker jumped out, moving quickly to my side to open the door. His gesture caught me off guard, but I didn't say anything, stepping out onto the pavement. The noise hit me first—a chaotic symphony of honking horns, overlapping conversations, and the low hum of life moving at full speed. Lights spilled from towering billboards, painting the streets and faces in neon blues, reds, and golds. People moved in every direction, a sea of strangers each carrying their own world.

I couldn't help but stare, my anger from earlier momentarily drowned by the sheer energy of it all. Times Square wasn't just a place—it was an experience. I felt small and significant all at once.

"It's something else, huh?" Booker's voice broke through my thoughts. He stepped closer, his hand reaching for mine.

My first instinct was to pull away, but I didn't. His hand was warm, grounding in the middle of all this chaos. I glanced down, surprised at how natural it felt. "Yeah," I said softly, allowing a small smile to creep onto my face. "It's amazing."

KITTEN HEELS

"Yeah, I know," he replied, a grin spreading across his face. "C'mon." He started leading me down the street, weaving us into the flow of tourists and locals alike. "Anything you want, everywhere you ever dreamed of being—it's all right here, shorty."

I followed him, his words rolling over me as we moved through the crowd. For a moment, I forgot about Bird, Hakeem, and everything else waiting for me outside this bubble. It was just me, Booker, and the city.

We stopped in front of a shop window, the mannequins dressed in sleek designer outfits that looked like they belonged on a runway. The reflection of the lights on the glass made it feel almost magical. My eyes lingered on a pair of Christian Louboutin heels—sharp, strappy, and red-soled. They weren't just shoes; they were a statement.

"You like those?" Booker asked, his voice close to my ear.

"They're nice," I replied, my voice soft as I studied them. I could already picture how they'd look on me—elevated, commanding.

"Well, go get them then," Booker said, his tone so casual it threw me off.

I turned to him, raising an eyebrow. "What?"

"You heard me." He tugged on my hand, pulling me toward the entrance of Barney's. "Go get them. Don't even think twice."

As we stepped inside, the shift was palpable. Eyes followed us, some curious, others blatantly skeptical. My back straightened, my chin lifting slightly in defiance. Booker leaned in close, his voice low but firm. "Don't let them get in your head, baby girl. They ain't used to us up in here, but we belong just as much as they do. Look at you—you look good."

I felt a blush creeping up my neck at his words, and I hated how much they affected me. I glanced at him, his confidence so natural, and felt some of it rub off on me.

I broke away from his hand, my eyes catching on the same pair of red-bottomed heels I'd seen in the window. Loubi Queens. I picked one up, running my fingers over the smooth leather before flipping it over to check the price: $875.

I set it down quickly, walking back toward Booker. "Not happening."

"You're not gonna get them?" he asked, his grin tugging at the corners of his mouth.

"Booker, those things cost almost $900!" I hissed, keeping my voice low.

"And?" He laughed, shaking his head. "You are Mickey Fuckin' Collins. You can have whatever you want. And if you can't, I got you."

I felt my face heat again, a blush I couldn't stop even if I tried. For a moment, I wondered if he meant it—if he really cared, or if this was just some game. His hand found mine again, his palm slightly sweaty but his grip steady. I wanted to argue, but his face was soft, genuine, and it threw me off balance.

I glanced down at my purse, remembering the stack of cash Hakeem had given me—fifteen, maybe twenty grand. I could buy the shoes ten times over if I wanted to, but I hadn't brought it all. I'd only tucked a few hundred in my bag before leaving the apartment, thinking I wouldn't need much for today. I wasn't about to blow the little I had on me on shoes, no matter how good they'd look on my feet.

Still, the thought of relying on Booker for anything made me hesitate. What was his game? Why was he doing all this for me? And why did it feel so… genuine?

Before I could decide, Booker waved down an employee. "Can she get these in a 7 or 7.5?" he asked.

The woman nodded quickly and disappeared into the back.

"How'd you know my size?" I asked, narrowing my eyes at him.

He smirked. "I'm good at sizing people up."

The shoes fit perfectly. Sliding them on, I felt an unfamiliar surge of confidence. I stood taller, my reflection in the mirror showing a woman who looked like she belonged here. But as quickly as the feeling came, it faded. I wasn't sure if I wanted to spend what little cash I had on something so extravagant.

"Can you hold these at the front for us?" Booker asked the employee before I could decide. He handed her the shoes, his tone leaving no room for argument.

We spent the next hour wandering the store, picking out clothes and accessories. Booker insisted on buying everything, brushing off my protests with a simple, "I got it." When we finally walked out, our arms were loaded with bags, and I couldn't help but feel a mix of gratitude and confusion. What was his angle? Why was he doing all this for me?

The night continued as we strolled through the streets, adding more bags to our collection. By the time we reached Central Park, the city had transformed into a quiet, glittering oasis. The park was beautiful at night, the air crisp and cool. I spotted a bench up ahead and quickened my pace, my arms aching from the weight of the bags.

Booker joined me as I sank onto the bench with a sigh of relief. "Not bad, huh?" he asked, leaning back and stretching his legs out in front of him.

"Not bad," I admitted, a small smile playing on my lips.

Before I could say more, his phone buzzed. He answered quickly, his tone shifting to something more serious. "Yeah. Alright. One," he said before hanging up.

"I gotta run," he said, standing. "But I've got a brownstone just up the street. You can stay there for the night. Make yourself at home."

I hesitated, the words catching in my throat. "Okay," I said finally, surprising even myself.

The walk to his place was quiet, the kind of silence that felt natural, not forced. When we arrived, he gave me a quick tour, his home warm and lived-in. It wasn't extravagant like Hakeem's, but it felt real. Safe.

"Here," he said, holding out my phone after punching in his number. "Call me if you need anything."

Then, before I could react, he leaned in and pressed a kiss to my cheek.

It wasn't a lingering kiss, but it was soft enough to send a ripple through me. My cheeks burned as I watched him walk out the door.

His place was nice—not flashy or overdone, but warm, lived-in, like every piece of furniture had its own story. It wasn't like Hakeem's sterile display of wealth, where everything was for show. This place had an ease to it. The brown leather sectional, the worn edges of the coffee table, even the faint scent of cedar in the air—it all felt like a home. It felt like his home.

For the first time in what felt like forever, I let myself relax. My shoulders softened as I sank into the couch, pulling my knees up under me. The remote rested on the armrest, almost inviting me to take control, and I did. I clicked the TV on, flipping through channels until I landed on an episode of Martin. Jerome was in the middle of saving Pam from a convenience store robbery, and within seconds, I was laughing out loud, the tension of the day momentarily forgotten.

"Jerome is so damn stupid," I muttered to myself, grinning as the scene unfolding.

Somehow, without even realizing it, my fingers had found my phone, dialing a number that was muscle memory by now. The ringing tone filled the room, and for a second, I hesitated. But before I could hang up, the line connected.

"Hello?" Ms. Fields' warm, familiar voice came through, and a wave of comfort washed over me.

"Hi Ms. Fields, it's Mickey. Is Carmen home?"

"Mickey! Chile, we been so worried about you! Where you

at? Are you okay?" Her concern was genuine, her voice laced with relief and worry, and it made something in my chest tighten.

Ms. Fields had always been that steady presence in my life, the kind of mom I used to dream about having. She worked long hours and struggled like the rest of us, but she was there. For Carmen. For me. She made sure we were fed, that we laughed, that we felt like we mattered. Talking to her now felt like slipping into an old, comfortable sweater.

"I'm fine, Ms. Fields. ACS placed me with my father." The words came out flat, and I could hear the skepticism in her pause.

"You mean Hakeem?!" She practically shouted, her disbelief loud enough to make me pull the phone away from my ear.

"Yes ma'am," I replied dryly, the corners of my mouth twitching in a reluctant smile.

"Oh my…" she started, but before she could continue, Carmen's voice cut in.

"I got it, ma!" Carmen's voice carried through the receiver, followed by the click of another line. "Hey Mick."

"Hey girl, what's up?" My voice softened, the weight of the day lifting slightly at the sound of her.

"Nothing. Chillin'. Sorry about moms—she's been on edge ever since you got snatched up outside of school. We didn't know what to think. Where you at?"

I hesitated for a moment, looking around Booker's brownstone, the realization of where I was settling over me like a strange, surreal wave. "Girl, you wouldn't believe me if I told you."

"Where girl, where?!" Carmen's voice rose with excitement, her tone pulling a small laugh out of me.

"Manhattan," I said quietly, the word feeling foreign on my tongue. Saying it out loud made it real. I was in Manhattan. Not in the projects. Not scraping by. But in a brownstone, surrounded by luxury and a kind of quiet I wasn't used to.

"Manhattan!" Carmen shrieked, her disbelief echoing through the phone. "What you doing in Manhattan?" she whispered, as if saying it any louder might jinx it.

I couldn't help but smile, even as the absurdity of it all hit me again. "I'll tell you everything. But listen—hop on the train and come meet me when your moms leaves for work. She's still pulling those double shifts at Lucky's Diner, right?"

"Yeah, she's getting ready to leave in a minute," Carmen said, her voice matter-of-fact but tinged with curiosity.

"Okay, cool. Write down this address. Take the C-Train, and then grab a cab to bring you the rest of the way. I'll be waiting for you outside."

There was a pause as she scribbled down the directions, and for a moment, I could hear the faint hum of the TV in the background, Jerome's ridiculous antics filling the silence. It was strange how something as simple as a show could tie me to Carmen, to a part of my life that felt so far away now. But it wasn't gone. Not completely.

"I got it," Carmen said finally, her voice steady. "I'll see you soon, Mick."

"See you soon," I replied, ending the call and setting the phone down beside me.

The couch cradled me as I leaned back, staring at the ceiling. The day had been a whirlwind, a mix of anger, confusion, and small moments of warmth I didn't quite know how to process. But as I sat there, in a space that felt more like a home than anywhere I had ever been, I let myself breathe. Just for a moment.

Jerome's voice crackled through the TV, pulling another laugh from me as I settled in, allowing the noise in my head to quiet.

10

After finishing the rest of *Martin* and laughing through the first half of *Sanford and Son*, I decided to head downstairs to wait for Carmen. The fresh evening air greeted me as I stepped out onto the stoop, the streetlights casting a warm glow over the quiet block. Just as I perched on the top step, I spotted a yellow cab pulling up. Perfect timing.

I jogged down the stairs, pulling a twenty-dollar bill from my pocket to hand to the driver through the passenger window. Before I could step back, the door swung open, and Carmen tumbled out like a burst of energy.

"Mickey! Girl, look how clean and quiet these streets is! ACS put you with a rich white foster family?!" she hollered, her words spilling out all at once as she slammed the car door shut and wrapped me in a tight hug. It was the kind of hug that made me feel like someone was holding me together, just when I felt like I might fall apart.

I laughed, shaking my head. "Hell no, girl," I whispered, trying to keep her volume in check. "Why would you even think that?"

She pulled back, giving me a playful side-eye before fully taking me in. Her hands landed on my shoulders as she inspected me from head to toe. "Oh my God, look at your hair… And your clothes. Those kicks are dope!" She stepped back, her hands on her hips, nodding like she was proud. "Yo, you like a real fly girl now."

Her words pulled a smile out of me, even as I tried to play it cool. I struck a little pose, tossing my hair over my shoulder. "Yeah, yeah, okay. Enough. C'mon, Car, I got a lot to tell you."

Inside, I sat cross-legged on the floor, Carmen's fingers flying through my hair as she attempted to recreate a style she'd seen in Ebony magazine. The feel of her tugging gently at my scalp was oddly comforting, soothing me as I laid it all out—the chaos of the past few days. I told her everything: my mom geeking out, the run in with the cop, the social workers, Hakeem's mansion, Bird's bullshit, and Booker, of course. I didn't hold back, pouring out every little detail, as if saying it all out loud would help me make sense of it.

When I finally finished, Carmen paused, tilting my head to the side as she inspected her work. "Dang, Mick," she said softly. "This is crazy."

I sighed, my shoulders sinking with the weight of it all. "Tell me about it," I muttered, feeling a strange mix of exhaustion and relief. Getting it out, even to just one person, made me feel a little lighter.

Carmen tapped my shoulder, signaling that she was done. "I

say make the most out of it, ya know? The fly girl life is better than the life you were living a couple days ago."

Pulling myself up from the sheepskin rug, I walked over to the circular platinum mirror hanging on the wall. The reflection staring back at me was a hood princess, styled to perfection. Carmen had braided the top part of my hair into two buns, letting strands dangle down, while the rest fell over my shoulders in soft waves. She really had a gift—she could recreate any hairstyle.

"Girl, this my song!" Carmen hollered suddenly.

I turned to see her turning up the volume on the TV as 2Pac's How Do You Want It blared through the speakers. Without hesitation, we started dancing to the beat, our movements loose and free, our laughter filling the room. For the first time in days, I felt like myself again.

The song ended, but we kept singing the chorus, collapsing onto the sofa in a fit of laughter. My sides ached from laughing so hard, tears streaming down my face. Wiping them away, I opened my eyes—and froze.

Booker was standing there, leaning against the doorway, his arms crossed, a smirk tugging at the corner of his mouth.

Carmen gasped when she spotted him, sitting up straight and muting the TV in a rush.

"Y'all having fun, huh?" Booker asked, his voice filled with amusement as he mimicked our dance moves and exaggerated singing voices.

"This is Booker, Carmen," I said, rolling my eyes, though a

small smile crept onto my face despite myself.

"Don't stop on account of me," he teased, still grinning.

I grabbed a pillow from the couch and chucked it at him, aiming for his head. He caught it with ease, laughing as he placed it back on the sofa. The whole scene felt so natural, like we'd all known each other forever. The way Carmen looked between the two of us told me it must've seemed that way to her, too.

"Hey, Carmen," Booker said, extending his hand toward her.

She hesitated for a moment before shaking it, her expression cautious. "Hey," she replied, her voice soft.

Booker turned back to me, his tone shifting slightly. "I just came back to grab something real quick. Y'all keep doing your thing. I'll see you later."

He disappeared into his room, reemerging a few moments later empty-handed. I wasn't sure what he'd come for, but it didn't seem to matter. Before Carmen could start grilling me, I walked over to him, catching him at the door.

"Hey," I said quietly. "Thanks for being cool. You know, with me inviting my girl over and all. I didn't mean to overstep or anything."

He waved off my concern, his tone easy. "It's all good, shorty. If you're good, then I'm good."

And then, without warning, he reached out, gently pinching my chin between his thumb and forefinger. "I'll see you later," he said, his voice low and warm.

I froze, my breath catching as a blush crept up my neck.

His touch was brief, but it left a warmth that lingered even after he turned and walked out the door.

I stood there for a moment, staring at the spot where he'd been, my heart thudding in my chest. Carmen's voice snapped me out of it.

"Girl," she said, drawing the word out as she raised an eyebrow. "What is that?"

"Nothing," I said quickly, turning away to hide my face. "Nothing at all."

But even as I plopped back down on the couch, Carmen's curious gaze fixed on me, I couldn't shake the feel of his touch or the way he'd looked at me. For the first time in a long time, I felt something I couldn't quite name. And it terrified me.

11

"Aye. Yo shorty, get up."

Booker's voice cuts through the haze of sleep. I blink my eyes open, groggy from the late-night movie binge and fridge-raiding. Carmen and I had crashed right where we'd fallen asleep, sprawled on the couch like we were too tired to care about anything else.

"What time is it?" I mumble, rubbing my eyes, my voice thick with sleep.

"It's 7 AM. You gotta be at Stone's by 10. You and your girl go get cleaned up, and we'll grab some breakfast before we head over there."

Carmen stirs beside me, lifting her head slowly, eyes squinting at the light. Booker and I burst out laughing when we see her. Her hair is standing on end like she's just been electrocuted, and there's dried saliva streaking from the corner of her lip down to her cheek—evidence of the deep sleep she had.

"Did somebody say breakfast?" she mutters, her voice still half asleep.

"Yeah." Booker chuckles, unaffected. "Ya'll go get showered and changed, and we'll hit up this little café nearby."

La Café sits tucked in the corner of 5th and 6th Ave, a small haven amidst the chaos of the city. The sidewalks are busy with the usual mix of people—morning joggers, office workers hustling to start their day early, the occasional walk of shame survivor, and tourists eager to start ticking off their sightseeing list.

As we walk in, a man—a beggar—stumbles toward us. His clothes are tattered, and the stench of cheap liquor wafts up from him like a storm cloud. He holds out a cup, eyes vacant but somehow pleading.

Before I can even think, Booker pulls out a crisp hundred-dollar bill from his pocket and drops it into the man's cup. The crust built up in the crooks of his eyes flaked and tumbled down his nose as his eyes sparked and came back to life at the realization that he could retire for the rest of the day. His smile is crooked, but grateful, showing the few teeth, he has left.

"Thank you." He says, his voice deep and rough-sounding as he nods his head in appreciation. He hurried away, the hundred-dollar bill already tucked safely in his ragged coat.

The warm croissant I order is a revelation. The eggs, spinach, and bacon inside feel like comfort on a plate. I take a bite and feel my stomach finally filling up in a way that Pop Tarts or Beanie Weenies never did. It's a small but satisfying luxury.

Carmen takes her time with a stack of pancakes and a glass of orange juice, but once she's done, she lets us know she has to head back before her mom gets off work. Booker's already on it, running outside to hail her a cab. He pays the driver in advance, a silent gesture that feels bigger than just a ride.

Once Carmen's gone, it's just me and Booker. There's an odd, unspoken shift between us. Walking back to his place feels heavier, like the weight of something unacknowledged is hanging between us.

When we get there, I'm surprised to see that Booker had a Porsche 911 parked out front. I hop in beside him, and we drive through the morning traffic, weaving in and out of lanes with the kind of smooth confidence that comes with years of practice.

The closer we get to Hakeem's place, the tighter my chest feels. Every turn we take feels like stepping closer to a cage I'd just managed to escape. My stomach twists, the freedom of the past day slipping further away with each passing block.

"You good shorty?" Booker's voice cuts through my spiraling thoughts, his eyes flicking toward me briefly before returning to the road.

I open my mouth to finally tell him to quit calling me "shorty" when he slams on the brakes. My body jerks forward against the seatbelt as a businessman in a gray suit darts into the street, briefcase clutched to his side like it holds the answers to the universe. Completely oblivious, he barrels into the middle of traffic, ignoring the cars screeching to a halt around him.

Booker slams the horn, the sharp sound cutting through the air. The businessman flips us off without breaking stride, narrowly avoiding a taxi and nearly getting taken out by a messenger on a bike.

Booker lets out a low whistle, shaking his head as we watch the man disappear onto the sidewalk. "These folks out here got a death wish," he mutters, his hand back on the wheel. A grin breaks across his face, and the sound of my laughter fills the car before I can stop it. The absurdity of it all—the businessman's nerve, the near collisions—it's too much.

As the laughter dies down, Booker leans back in his seat, one hand casually gripping the wheel. "Man, New York. Ain't no place like it."

We keep driving, the city blurring past us in streaks of movement and sound. Booker starts talking about his dreams, his plans to create something that matters. "I'm telling you, shorty, Black Wall Street wasn't just an idea. It was a blueprint. Tulsa's Greenwood District? That was power, and they knew it. That's why they burned it down. But I'm bringing it back. Modern, unapologetic, and ours."

The conviction in his voice is magnetic. The way he speaks, like there's no room for failure in his vision, draws me in. I can't help but admire the passion burning in him, the way his mind works in layers I'm only beginning to understand.

A strange warmth spreads through me, unbidden but undeniable. It starts small, then grows, spreading like a ripple until it settles somewhere deep. I try to ignore it, to focus on the city outside the window, but the fluttering in my chest only grows stronger.

I crack the window, letting the rush of cool air sweep in and settle against my skin. Inhale. Exhale. Keep it together, Mick.

"So…" The word slips out before I can stop it. "You got a girlfriend?" My voice is too casual, the question too forced, and I immediately regret it.

Booker's head tilts slightly, and I catch the hint of a smirk forming on his lips. My cheeks burn, and I reach for the radio, cranking up the volume to drown out my embarrassment. Wendy Williams' voice fills the silence, giving me something else to focus on.

"You asking for you or just making conversation?" Booker's voice cuts through Wendy's chatter, smooth and teasing.

I glance at him from the corner of my eye, refusing to give him the satisfaction of a full response. "I'm just curious," I mutter, sinking a little lower in my seat.

Booker chuckles softly, and the sound stirs something in me that I wish it didn't. "Nah, no girlfriend," he says, his tone easy but deliberate. "Ain't found anyone worth the time yet."

The warmth in his words lingers in the air, unspoken but heavy. I stare out the window, trying to focus on anything but him, but the smile tugging at the corners of my mouth betrays me.

Booker doesn't push further, letting the moment hang lightly between us as we glide through the streets. But as the car turns into Hakeem's building, I feel a wave of dread. The conversation, the laughter, the fluttering—all of it fades into the cold reality waiting for me outside this car.

The fingerprinting process was surprisingly quick and efficient. As I pressed my fingers against the scanner and watched the machine record my prints, I couldn't help but feel the weight of everything that had brought me here. Yesterday's chaos seemed far away now, replaced by the dull routine of bureaucratic necessity. Still, I kicked myself for not making it in time then—it would've saved me a whole lot of trouble.

Thomas was polite, as usual, though his stiff demeanor didn't waver much. When he handed me a slim white key card, he explained in his steady tone, "This will allow you access to the building after it locks up at 10 PM. You're officially in the system now, Miss Collins. You can come and go as you please."

I took the card, feeling its smooth surface between my fingers, and nodded. The words "come and go as you please" lingered in my mind, but they didn't bring the freedom I hoped for. Not yet.

As we walked back toward the lobby, Booker strolled casually beside me, hands stuffed into his pockets, his stride as easy as ever. He and Thomas exchanged light conversation, something about traffic uptown and a Knicks game that Booker couldn't stop clowning on. I chimed in occasionally, but my focus was elsewhere—on the penthouse waiting above me and the invisible pressure building with every step closer.

When we reached the lobby, Booker turned to me, his dark eyes holding that steady gaze of his. "You want me to come up with you?" he asked, his voice casual but with an undertone that made my pulse quicken. It wasn't just a question—it was a quiet offer of support, of something I wasn't sure how to accept.

I hesitated, shifting the key card in my hand. The idea of having him with me was tempting, but I couldn't let myself lean on him. Not right now. I needed to keep my footing steady, to face this new life on my own terms. "Nah, I'm good," I said, trying to keep my voice light. "Ain't you got somewhere to be?"

It was an obvious excuse, and we both knew it. I could see it in the slight arch of his brow, the flicker of amusement that tugged at the corner of his mouth. But he didn't call me on it. He just nodded, his easy grin softening into something quieter.

"Alright, shorty," he said, his tone warm but measured. "But you know where I'm at if you need me."

I nodded, swallowing against the lump in my throat. "Thanks, Book," I murmured, glancing away to avoid the weight of his gaze. I didn't want him to see the conflict stirring behind my eyes, the way being around him made my thoughts scatter like leaves in the wind.

He stepped back, giving me space without pressing further. "Catch you later, then," he said, his voice laced with a subtle reassurance that lingered even as he turned to leave.

I watched him go, his figure disappearing through the glass doors of the lobby. A part of me wanted to call him back, to let him walk with me, stand with me, take some of the weight I was carrying. But I didn't. I clutched the key card tighter in my hand and turned toward the elevator.

As the doors slid shut behind me, sealing me inside the metal box, I took a deep breath and tried to steady the racing thoughts in my head. Booker was starting to feel like something solid, something real, and that scared me more than anything waiting for me upstairs.

This was my life now, and I had to face it alone. Or at least, that's what I'm telling myself.

12

The elevator doors slide open with a soft chime, and I step into the penthouse foyer. The air is thick with tension before I even take a step. Hakeem's voice booms, sharp and commanding, as he paces the room, arguing heatedly with someone over the phone. His words are clipped, his tone icy, like a man used to getting what he wants.

I keep my head low, trying to make myself small, invisible. I don't want his attention. I just want to make it to my room, close the door, and drown out the world for a while. But, of course, I'm not that lucky.

"Hold up," Hakeem barks, cutting his phone call short. His voice halts me mid-step, and I can feel the weight of his gaze pressing down on me. Slowly, I turn, my fingers tightening around the shopping bags in my hands.

"I see you found your way back," he says, his eyes narrowing as he looks me over, like he's assessing me for damage. "Where you stay last night?"

The question lands like a slap, sharp and accusatory. I shrug, trying to brush it off, but his tone digs under my skin, igniting something raw inside me.

"Like you care," I mutter, my voice low but venomous. The words spill out before I can stop them, and the moment they do, regret coils tight in my chest. I've already pushed too far. Fear flashes in my mind like a warning light, but I try to mask it. I grab the bags tighter and turn away, heading toward my room in silence.

"Mickey," he calls after me, his footsteps heavy as he follows. "Look, I'm your daddy, but I'm not your daddy."

The words hit me like a brick, stopping me cold. My body stiffens, and my heart pounds in my chest. What does that even mean? I turn my head slightly, just enough to catch him in my peripheral vision.

He steps closer, arms folded across his chest, his stance firm and unyielding. "There's no emotional connection there," he says, his voice flat. "I mean I never really felt like your father. I'm just a man taking care of you 'cause your moms ain't right right now."

The man who carries himself as the king of the streets, with his tailored suits and smooth speeches, suddenly feels small—a coward hiding behind his indifference. His words strip away any illusion I might have held about what this relationship could be.

"I'm not gonna hold your hand," he continues, his tone like ice. "Nobody's gonna fuck with you 'cause you're my seed, but don't think I'm going to be out here coddling you."

His words linger in the air, sharp and cutting. They slice

through me, each syllable a reminder of how alone I am. I grip the handles of my shopping bags tighter, my knuckles white with tension. The sting of his apathy settles deep, far beyond the surface.

I move again, forcing my feet forward until I reach my room. Tossing the bags into the closet, I slam the door shut with more force than I intend, the sound reverberating through the penthouse. My hands tremble slightly as I press them against the door, trying to steady myself, trying to push down the anger and hurt bubbling to the surface.

But he's not done. His voice carries through the crack of the door, heavy and unrelenting. "You hear me, Mickey? Ain't no fairy tales here. You don't need me to hold your hand. Handle your shit."

I press my forehead against the cool wood, his words weighing on me like lead, cold and unyielding. The permanence of it washes over me, stealing my breath for a fleeting moment.

Slowly, I turn and open the door. He's standing there, his face hard, his eyes searching mine for something—submission, understanding, maybe even defiance. I give him none of it. Instead, I lift my chin, meeting his gaze head-on. My silence speaks louder than any argument could.

His eyes drop for a moment, the slightest hesitation breaking through his steely exterior. It's fleeting, but it's enough. Enough for me to know that I don't need his approval, his affection, or his version of fatherhood. I don't need him at all.

"Got it," I say finally, my voice steady and emotionless. "You don't need to worry about me."

I step back into my room, closing the door firmly behind me, shutting him out. My chest heaves as I exhale slowly, the power of the exchange pressing down on me like a vice. I lean against the door, my head tilted back, staring at the ceiling as the reality sinks in.

Hakeem and I—we're just two people bound by blood and circumstance. There's no warmth, no connection, no love. He's stone, and I'm learning to be the same.

13

It had been two weeks since Hakeem left for his so-called "business trip" to Canada. It was just me, Bird, and an occasional pop up from Booker. Bird and I had patched things up after she decided to play diplomat—showing up uninvited and demanding Thomas let her up when I dodged her calls. Apparently, she got tired of me freezing her out over her disappearing act with Trev.

The past week had been an education. A crash course in everything street. I learned who the players were—from the top dogs to the nickel baggers. I picked up the rules of the game, the cost of doing business, who paid who, and when collections were due. Bird didn't waste time letting the world know: I wasn't just Hakeem "Stone" Collins' daughter. I was the new princess of the streets. From Staten Island to the Bronx, everyone knew my name.

The shift was surreal. Women who once carried themselves like queens, flashing their dealer boyfriends' cash, now whispered my name in hushed tones. I soaked it all in. The power trickled over me like a baptism, covering me from head to toe. But I kept a leash on it. Taking too much in—letting it rule me—was a trap. One I wasn't about to fall into. I would play the part, but I wouldn't let the game take me.

By now, I had mastered the art of dressing like a boss, talking like a boss. Word was law, and anyone who came up short paid the price. I learned the business inside and out: Hakeem controlled the cocaine and heroin game with product from the Medellín Duro Cartel, while Los Zaptas kept a steady stream of marijuana flowing. The Italians ran the gun trade, and the local riffraff managed the prostitutes. Every dollar exchanged, every wire transferred, Hakeem got his cut. And by extension, so did I.

"Here are your latest reports, Miss Collins." Tyler McPhee slid a folder across the table, his hands shaking slightly as if he'd just delivered a treasure chest to a pirate queen.

I had him meet me at Mavis Tapas and Tavern for our weekly meeting. I never use the same spot twice. Couldn't have anyone thinking these were just business meetings—not when drugs and cash were involved.

Fourteen years old and two hundred grand saved. In just two weeks, I'd racked up more money than most people saw in a lifetime. Tyler, a Wall Street broker—one of Hakeem's high-profile clients—helped me set up an untraceable bank account. He needed his "medication" and buying from anyone less than the boss was beneath him. With Hakeem out of town, that left me. Lanky, with dark eyes and jittery hands, he'd do anything to stay in my good graces. And since he handled money—my ticket out—I'd do anything to stay in his.

"I took the liberty of investing 50% of this week's revenue into some stocks and bonds for you," Tyler offered, sliding another folder over. A quick glance showed names like Apple, Disney, and something called Qualcomm. I stuffed the paperwork into my purse and handed him a small duffle bag from my side.

"Here you go, Tyler. As always, it's been a pleasure." I stood to leave, strapping my purse over my shoulder.

"Miss Collins, wait." He grabbed my arm, halting my movement.

"The Qualcomm and Apple stocks are expected to triple your investment by the end of the week. I was hoping…" His voice trailed off, his confidence evaporating. He looked at the table like a child afraid to ask for a second helping. I knew what he wanted. More drugs.

I leaned down, cupping his face gently. "You take care of me, and I'll take care of you," I whispered, lifting his head until his eyes met mine. Giving him a wink, I reached into my purse and pulled out an eight ball I'd planned to give to Rice Cake, my ear to the streets. Holding it tightly, I got close enough for my words to sting. "But the next time you invest my money without running it past me, NYPD will be fishing you out of the Hudson."

He nodded frantically, and I let him go. As I walked out onto 14th Street, a car screeched to a stop in front of me. My hand instinctively went to the taser in my bag. The window rolled down, and I exhaled when I saw Booker behind the wheel.

"Mick! I been looking everywhere for you. Get in," he barked.

I slid into the car, his urgency gripping me before he even said a word. "What's going on?"

"Stone. Hakeem… He's been arrested."

The words hit like a slap, but not a surprise. I'd been preparing for this ever since I got pulled into his world. Every dollar saved, every move I made, was to brace for this. My hands tightened into fists, but my face stayed calm—lesson one in this life.

"What happened?"

"They picked him up crossing the Canadian border. Five hundred kilos."

Damn. What was he driving, a freight train? I shook my head as Booker weaved through traffic.

"We need to lay low," he said. "I'm taking you home to grab some things, and then we're out of here."

"Out of here? To where?" My heart pounded. If they'd been watching Hakeem, they knew about me. About Booker.

He must have read my mind. "I got you, Mick." He placed a reassuring hand on my thigh, but I wasn't convinced. I needed a plan of my own.

"First, take me to the Bank of New York."

Booker glanced at me like I'd lost my mind. "The bank? Did you not just hear what I said? We're getting out of town."

"And did you not just hear me? Bank. Now." My tone left no room for argument, and his scowl told me he knew it.

Minutes later, we pulled up to the bank. I darted inside, documents clutched tightly in my bag. I was in and out, we made it to Upper Echelon to get my things in no time.

"I'ma stay out here while you run up real quick and keep my eyes open." Booker states as we pull up, grabbing my arm as I open the door. "Be quick." He instructs with a stern look on face.

I get out and scurry inside to see Thomas talking to a gang of suits. DEA, FBI, and local cops were all in attendance. My chest tightened as their eyes landed on me.

Thomas's face was pale, his eyes darting nervously, but he couldn't meet mine. He looked like a man who'd already spilled everything he knew. My jaw clenched as realization set in.

Good thing I made that stop.

"Miss Collins," one of the agents said, stepping forward with a practiced smile that didn't reach his eyes. "We need to have a word. It's about your father."

Father. Why did everyone insist on using that word?

Before I could respond, they flanked me on both sides, escorting me out. I caught a glimpse of Booker in the car, his face twisting in fury as he slammed on the gas, leaving me behind.

And just like that, my world shifted again.

14

"Ma'am. Ma'am." A flight attendant nudges my shoulder, waking me from a restless sleep. Her bright smile feels like an intrusion.

I blink away the haze, my mind scrambling to catch up. We've landed at JFK. I must have dozed off, caught in the endless replay of my past. Sleep hasn't exactly been a luxury since the arrest. A bitch is tired.

The memories don't help. They churn and boil like water in a pot left too long on the stove. I still feel the chill from the day the feds snatched me up, fear clawing at my insides even though my game face never cracked. They didn't get a damn thing out of me.

My life shifted that day, but that's a story for later.

Dragging my carry-on through the terminal, I'm hit with the smell of greasy pizza and burnt coffee. The chaos of New York doesn't bother me—it feels like a wake-up call. The first person who comes to mind, unexpectedly, is Bird.

The thought of Bird softens something inside me. Maybe I'll stop by to see her before diving into my hunt for Raul—or whatever his real name is. The plan is to hit the ground running, but nostalgia has me by the throat. A quick ride through the old stomping grounds couldn't hurt, right?

At baggage claim, I pull out my phone and dial Turo to arrange a rental. Sure, I could grab something basic from Enterprise right here in the airport, but that's not me. Life's too short for mediocrity.

"Surprise me," I tell the Turo rep when they ask what kind of car I want.

And surprise me they do. Stepping through the automatic doors, I find a sleek 2025 Maserati Ghibli parked and waiting. The driver meets me halfway, handing over the keys with a polite smile.

"Thank you," I say, tilting my head slightly. "Do you mind loading my bags into the trunk?"

"Of course." He obliges, his movements quick and efficient.

Should I tip him? The thought lingers for a second before I brush it off. **Fuck him.**

Sliding into the car, I grip the wheel and feel the engine's purr beneath me. Time to move. Last I heard, Bird was staying in Brooklyn. The thought of her in the midst of gentrified madness brings a cynical smile to my lips.

Brooklyn isn't Brooklyn anymore. Instead of kids playing on the sidewalks, I see preppy white women walking designer dogs and shirtless men jogging in packs. Google Maps takes me to a familiar brownstone, its once-vivid exterior faded but intact. I climb the stoop and knock on the first-floor door.

Three knocks in, it swings open.

And there she is—Harriet Love Finley. My so-called mother.

The sight of her steals the air from my lungs. She's sober. Healthy-looking, even. But the hurt? It slams into me like a greyhound bus, stirring up every old wound I thought I'd buried.

"Yes, can I help you?" Her voice is light, her eyes scanning me like I'm a stranger. Like I'm nobody.

Disgusted, I force my jaw to work. "No." The word escapes like venom. I spin on my heel and walk away, my chest tight with a mix of rage and heartbreak.

I knew coming back here wouldn't be easy, but I didn't expect this. Love looked good—clean, polished. It made me sick. Why hadn't she reached out once she got her act together? The question twists inside me, but I don't know if I even want the answer.

Back in the car, I pause for a moment, scanning the windows. That's when I see her—standing behind the glass, watching me. Her eyes are heavy with something I can't place. Recognition? Regret?

Whatever it is, it's too late.

I throw on my shades, slam the door shut, and press the gas, the Maserati roaring in defiance. Fuck Harriet. Fuck Bird. Fuck all of them.

DVSN and Future's No Cryin' blares through the speakers, the perfect anthem for my mood. Windows down, music up, I let the rhythm push me forward. The city rushes past in a blur of steel and concrete, a bittersweet reminder of everything I've fought for—and lost.

By the time I cross the George Washington Bridge, I'm running on instinct. Something pulls me toward the suburbs. The light blue house with crisp white trim comes into view, and I pull into the driveway.

My pulse steadies as I ring the bell.

Little feet scurry on the other side, and with a second knock, the door swings open.

"Hey, Carmen."

15

Carmen Fields is my girl. Her house was a sanctuary for me back in the day. Ms. Fields, Carmen's mom, was a single mother like so many black women, always struggling but never asking questions. She'd open her doors and arms wide for me. Carmen never judged me either. She'd just scoot over, making room for me on her twin-sized bed.

Although our paths took us in different directions over the years, we always stayed in touch. Carmen had married a college professor and now had three kids. Seeing her face instantly brought me peace.

"Mickey?! What are you doing here?" Even though Carmen's tone was one of shock at seeing me on her doorstep, her face lit up with happiness.

"Girl, I just ended up here." I went in for a hug.

As we embraced, I heard little feet running toward us. I pulled away to see them—their tiny faces beaming with excitement.

"Auntie Mick! Auntie Mick!" The voices of my godchildren, Solomon, the oldest at five, and the three-year-old twins, Piper and Olivia, echoed.

"Hey Chipmunks!" I called out, scooping them up in a big hug, planting kisses on all three of them.

"All right, all right. Let Auntie Mick get inside before you all go crazy." Carmen stepped in, breaking up the commotion.

I showered the kids with more kisses before picking myself up from the floor.

"Tiffany!" Carmen suddenly called out.

A young white woman emerged from the kitchen. "Yes ma'am?"

"Tiffany, could you take the kids? I have a friend visiting; we'll be in the mom room."

"Yes ma'am." Tiffany, clearly the nanny, gathered the chipmunks. "Come now. Who wants a snack?"

"Me!" they shrieked in unison.

"C'mon, Mickey." Carmen led me through her home. I hadn't visited since she added a "mom room." She seemed excited to show me her new space.

Stopping at the side door, Carmen retrieved a set of keys from her pocket and unlocked it.

"Welcome." She opened the door, flashing a huge grin.

"Girl!" The basement had been completely transformed.

"I know, right!"

"This is fantastic!" I exclaimed, walking around the room. The entire wall was lined with wine bottles, a fully stocked bar, and plush velvet furniture filled the space with deep, inviting tones. The lighting was perfect, making it feel like a cozy lounge.

"I'd never leave." I admitted, plopping down on the sofa in front of the lit fireplace.

"I know, I love it. To be honest, I needed it." Carmen opens up to me. " I told Marcus, either give me a mom room or give me a divorce."

"I know that's right! And I see you got it!" We both laugh, slapping fives.

"A bitch needs a break!" She says, still laughing as she went to the bar to make us drinks.

She handed me a Grey Goose Martini she'd just prepared and sat down on the bearskin rug in front of the fire. Carmen reached into a vase on the side and pulled out a slim silver case along with a box of matches. She opened the case, revealing a joint, and after lighting it, took a long drag, inhaling deeply before exhaling.

"You know I love you, Mick, but what's up with this drive-by?"

I took the joint from her, taking a long steady pull before answering. "You won't believe what I've gotten myself into."

I spent the next hour and a half catching Carmen up on everything that had happened with Raul. By the time I finished my story of how I fell in love and got crossed, we had finished off two and a half bottles of wine and smoked two joints.

"What the hell are you gonna do, Mick?"

"I'm going to find his ass and fuck him up!" I spat. "The only thing is, he's not who he said he was, so I don't even know where to begin." I finished somberly.

"This shit is fucked up." Carmen said, shaking her head and popping a handful of popcorn into her mouth. "Did you get anything from the police when you spoke with them?"

I stood up from the sofa and began pacing the floor. The weed was making me focused as hell.

"You know what, yes. Yes, yes, yes. That's actually why I'm in the city." I reached down, picking up my glass and taking a sip. "When they were showing me all his mugshots, one said Rochester, New York. Maybe I can start there?"

"Okay, that's a start. And you know who's from Rochester and knows everybody, don't you?" She shook her finger at me, standing and going over to the vanity. She dug through a planning folder and pulled out a sticky note, writing something down.

"Oh, that's not going to happen."

"What other choice do you have, Mick?" Carmen retorted, handing me the paper. "Call him, you know he'll be more than willing to help."

"But Book though, bitch? We don't know anyone else from that way?" I snatched the sheet from her hand and plopped back down on the sofa, staring at the name and number intently.

Booker Colis Reed started out as the little kid who ran around with my dad but ended up being my first love. Hell, the one who pulled the last straw that made me say fuck it. It's not like I learned my lesson with Book; look at the predicament my ass is in now.

"I don't know, Carmen."

"What other choice do you have, Mick?" Carmen asked softly, sitting down on the arm of the sofa.

"I'll think about it." I managed, stuffing Booker's info into my back pocket. "What you cooking? A bitch is hungry." I changed the subject.

"Me too, hoe." We laughed at one another. "Come on, let's get Tiffany to cook us something."

16

"Auntie Mick! Auntie Mick! Wake up! Wake up!" Piper and Olivia jumped on me, shaking me awake. That white girl sure could cook! She whipped up pan-seared salmon, garlic mashed potatoes, and asparagus in no time. My sleepy ass must have caught the itis because I fell asleep on the living room floor.

"Hey, chipmunks, what time is it?" I mumbled groggily.

"We don't know," Piper giggled, jumping on me again and causing a groan to escape my lips.

"Okay, okay. I'm getting old, let me get up. Where's your mom?" I asked, pushing myself up from the floor.

"In the kitchen with Daddy," they both answered in unison, then began to jump on each other, chasing and giggling.

I made my way toward the kitchen, but as I got closer, I heard hushed voices. Someone didn't want to be overheard.

I stopped and tried to inch closer quietly, attempting to stay out of sight. Leaning against the wall, I listened intently, trying to make out the words.

"Why is she here, Carmen?" I heard Marcus's unmistakable voice, tinged with frustration.

"Marcus, this is my sister. Why wouldn't she be here?!" Carmen's voice was defensive, hurt even. I could understand Marcus's caution, though. The tension between them was palpable.

"Have you not seen the news?" he pressed. "You know what, I'm pretty sure she's already told you all about her criminal acts. We have children—what on earth were you thinking?!"

"Stop it, Marcus!" Carmen's voice trembled with anger. "This conversation is over. You can sleep on the couch tonight."

Before I knew it, Carmen was coming around the corner, almost running into me.

"I should go."

"Mickey, wait," Carmen called after me.

"No, Marcus is right. I shouldn't have come here, I'm sorry."

I pat my pockets to make sure I had my keys and phone, not feeling them. I began to look around the living room, my heart pounding.

"You don't have to leave; he just doesn't understand." She begins to walk after me.

I stop and look my friend in the eyes. "I shouldn't have bought my drama to your door Car. I'm not even sure if the Feds are still watching me, I don't want you guys to be involved. You got out the life." I reason, pointing around her home and at my sweet godchildren so she could really understand.

I spot my keys and phone laying on one of the end tables.

"I'll keep you posted." I grab my things and plant a kiss on her cheek before heading for the front door.

Carmen grabbed my arm and turned me back toward her, embracing me in a tight hug. "Call him, Mick." She whispered in my ear.

Without another word, I walked out, the weight of her words heavy on my heart.

17

I appreciated Carmen having my back, but Marcus was right. The last thing I wanted was for her or her family to get tangled up in my mess.

The sun was setting, and I hadn't accomplished a single thing I came here to do. Crossing the bridge back into the city, I pulled my phone out at the first red light and dialed.

"This is Sandra."

"Sandra, it's Mickey."

"Mickey, darling! How are you?"

"I'm fine, thanks."

"Well, tell me—what brings the pleasure of hearing from you?"

Sandra Perkins—managing partner of Perkins & Stevens, one of the top law firms in New York City, and an old friend. She was always straight to business, no time wasted. Not when money could be made.

"Listen, I need to meet," I said, cutting to the chase.

"Yes, let's. I'll be finished here in an hour. Le Coucou?"

"My hotel's easier. Room service is on me. I'm at the Four Seasons Downtown, Barclay Suite."

"Got it. See you soon, hon."

I hung up and hit the gas as the light turned green. By the time I got checked in and made it to my suite, the stress was finally catching up to me. Dropping my bags at the door, I took in my surroundings. For $3,000 a night, the room was immaculate—everything I needed and then some.

Heading straight to the bathroom, I turned the faucet on and sprinkled in the provided bath salts and bubble foam. While the water filled the tub, I called room service and ordered one of everything from the menu, plus a pitcher of orange juice and a bottle of champagne.

Ending the call, I pick it right back up.

"Front desk."

"This is Mickey Collins, I'm expecting Sandra Perkins. Please send her up when she arrives."

"Yes ma'am."

I connected my phone to the room's Bluetooth system and queued up Anita Baker on Pandora. As her sultry voice filled the space, I slipped into the tub. The hot water hit me like a balm, melting the tension from my shoulders. I sank deeper and let the music wash over me.

Anita's voice crooned through the suite:

"Turning back the hands of time, holding on to misty memories…"

The melody tore through me, unearthing everything I'd

buried. First came the slow tears, rolling down my cheeks like a quiet drizzle. But soon, they were waterfalls, pouring out years of pain, heartbreak, and frustration. It wasn't just Raul—it was everything. Memories I thought I'd buried came flooding back, like a stampede trampling through my mind.

I thought I was healed.

I thought I was over this.

But there I was, ugly crying in a tub, feeling raw and stupid. I'd believed Raul was different, that he loved me for me, that my wallet-chasing days were over. I thought I'd found my person.

It was all a lie.

Wiping my face, I dunked my head underwater, letting the shock jolt me back to reality. Climbing out, I grabbed a towel and faced myself in the mirror. My eyes were red, my cheeks blotchy, but the anger bubbling inside overpowered my sadness.

"Get it together, bitch," I told my reflection, placing my hands firmly on the sides of the sink. "You're Mickey fucking Collins."

I stared myself down until I believed it, then wrapped myself in the plush robe and went to unpack. Sliding on a sleek black Tom Ford bodycon dress, I smoothed my hair and applied my makeup. The bad bitch was emerging.

A knock at the door signaled room service. Five men rolled in with carts, arranging everything meticulously.

"Do you need anything else, Ms. Collins?" one asked.

"No, thank you," I said, handing him a crisp hundred-dollar bill. "Split this."

They nodded and left, leaving me with a buffet fit for royalty. I popped open the champagne but quickly realized I needed something stronger. Grabbing a mini bottle of Tito's from the bar, I tipped it back in one gulp before finally fixing a mimosa.

As SWV's "Weak" started playing, I caught a glimpse of myself in the mirror. I looked good—damn good. The phone rang, interrupting my moment.

"Yes?"

"Ms. Collins, Sandra Perkins is requesting access."

"Send her up," I said, irritated. Didn't I tell them to let her through?

I touch up my Mac Russian Red lipstick as Sandra knocks.

"Sandra, darling!" I greeted her, kissing both cheeks.

"Mickey, it's been too long," she replied. Her heels click as she enters, shrugging off her peach blazer and draping it over the chaise.

"Help yourself," I said, gesturing to the spread.

After piling her plate high, Sandra settled onto the chaise where she'd left her blazer. She popped a grape into her mouth and started speaking, her words muffled by the fruit.

"Listen, I know why I'm here."

"You do?" I asked, raising an eyebrow.

"Oh, absolutely." She chewed, then smirked. "I haven't heard from you in what—eight, nine years? And even then, it was because you were fundraising for that police commissioner in Atlanta. So, naturally, I knew this call wasn't a social one. I did my research."

Of course, she did. Sandra was always about her business, one step ahead at all times. I shouldn't have expected anything less. I drained the rest of my mimosa, feeling the weight of her words settle over me like a heavy cloak. Fuck this. I got up, walked to the bar, and grabbed two mini bottles of Tito's. Since Sandra was here, I poured them into a glass instead of chugging straight from the bottle and took a slow sip.

"So, how bad do you think it is, San?" I asked, turning to face her. She was already back at the buffet, this time going for the gourmet chicken wings and sliders. Apparently, she'd moved on to her entrée.

"I'm not sure yet," she replied, spearing a chicken wing with a fork. "But it sounds bad. Really bad. I won't know for sure until I see what the FBI has. I assume this meeting means you're hiring me?"

"Absolutely. This whole thing is absurd!" I downed another big gulp of vodka, letting the burn cut through my rising anxiety.

Sandra finally set her plate down on the end table, her demeanor shifting. "Mick, sit down. Come here."

Her tone was firm but not cold, her eyes carrying a flicker of genuine concern. I hesitated, then sat across from her. She leaned forward, resting her elbows on her knees.

"These are serious accusations," she said. "If you're charged and convicted, you could be looking at 14 years in federal prison. And that's just for the money laundering."

The air in the room seemed to freeze. My stomach dropped.

Sandra got up, bypassed the champagne entirely, and went to the bar, pouring herself a Jameson neat. That alone told me how serious this was.

"The good news," she continued, turning back to me, "is that no charges have been filed yet. But even so, this kind of thing can ruin your reputation—and your business—if it's not handled carefully."

"And that is the last thing I need!" I snapped, frustration bubbling to the surface. "I've worked too damn hard to get where I am. I can't let everything I've built be destroyed because of my poor choice in men."

Sandra nodded, her expression neutral but understanding. "I'll start by sending a cease-and-desist to the agent in charge of the case. I'll demand they keep your name out of any public mention unless you're formally charged. That'll buy us some time."

The tension in my chest eased slightly. I wasn't sure if it was the liquor kicking in or the fact that Sandra made it sound like she had everything under control. "Thanks, San," I murmured, sinking back into the sofa.

"Sure thing, doll." She grabbed her blazer and slipped it on, smoothing the sleeves. "By the way, have you gone to see Jacob since you've been back?"

Her question hit me like a slap. Of all the names she could've brought up. "No," I said flatly, closing my eyes as I leaned back. The room swayed slightly. Yep, I was drunk.

"He can help, Mick," she said, her voice softer now. She

reached out and patted my leg. I lifted my head just enough to meet her gaze. She was right, of course, but I wasn't in the mental space to admit it—not even to myself.

Sandra stood, smoothing her blazer again. "I've got to go now, Mikayla. My work is never done."

I got up and walked her to the door. She turned to face me, leaning in to kiss both my cheeks. "We'll talk soon," she said, pulling me into a light hug.

Before letting her go, I blurted, "San, you know I didn't do this, right?"

She paused, then smirked. "Babe, as long as the check clears, I don't care." Winking, she stepped into the hallway. "Oh, that reminds me. Retainer fee: $200K. I'll give you a couple of days. I'll go ahead and send the cease-and-desist, but that's as far as I go without payment."

"No problem. I'll get the wire started," I assured her.

"Good." She gave me one last smile. "Be safe, Mick. I'll call you tomorrow." With that, she was gone.

As the door clicked shut, I leaned against it and exhaled. Sandra didn't play. Not with her time, not with her words, and certainly not with her money.

18

I didn't sleep worth a damn last night. It's like I'm stuck in limbo—caught between the past and the present, unable to move forward. No matter how hard I try, the truth is clear: I can't step into my future until I make peace with my past. It's the key to untangling the mess I'm in now.

First things first—I need to see an old friend.

Picking up the hotel phone, I dial zero while grabbing the remote from the coffee table. As it rings, I turn on the TV. CNN sparks to life. I leave it there, the hum of the news filling the empty space.

"Room service," a cheerful voice answers.

"Good morning. Can I get a pot of coffee, and the Presidential Breakfast sent up?"

Yes, I ordered the works: scrambled eggs, bacon, hashbrowns, grits, fruit, French toast, champagne, and orange juice. For the record, yes, grits exist up north. And yes, I'm about to eat like royalty—don't judge me.

"Absolutely! Right away, Ms. Collins," the receptionist replies, their enthusiasm jolting me awake.

I sigh, dragging myself off the couch to find something to wear. My plan is to head to Yorkville, but as I'm digging through my suitcase, the news anchor's voice grabs my attention.

"We're cutting to breaking news out of Atlanta, Georgia. Conner, what's going on at the Fulton County Courthouse?"

I freeze mid-step, my attention snapping to the screen. The camera shifts to a field reporter standing outside the courthouse, the caption below reading: FBI Press Conference – RICO Case Update.

"Yes, Beth," the reporter says. "I'm live at the Fulton County Courthouse, where Agent Sharon Cochran has called an unexpected press conference. While the purpose hasn't been disclosed, we believe it relates to the high-profile RICO case involving Raul Santiago, also known as Jason Montgomery, and Fancy Me Boutique owner, Mikayla Collins."

My blood turns to ice at the mention of Raul's name. My feet feel bolted to the floor, but I force myself forward, collapsing onto the couch. I grab the remote and crank up the volume, my heart pounding in my ears.

The camera cuts to an empty podium on the courthouse steps. Moments later, Agent Cochran emerges, clutching a single sheet of paper. She's wearing the same tired navy suit as before, looking just as smug as I remember.

"I've called this press conference to address the national

attention surrounding wanted fugitive Jason Montgomery," Cochran begins, her tone clipped and matter-of-fact.

Jason Montgomery. The name slices through me like a blade.

Cochran continues, her words sharp and deliberate. "I want to be clear: Mikayla 'Mickey' Collins is not a suspect in this case. Jason Montgomery—let me repeat that name—Jason Montgomery. He is wanted for money laundering, fraud, and felony identity theft, among other charges. Ms. Collins was briefly detained to assist in the investigation but is not a person of interest at this time."

I release a shaky breath, my mind reeling. Sandra doesn't play. If this is what her cease-and-desist looks like, I can only imagine what she's capable of. I am making a mental note to confirm that wire transfer—$200K well spent.

"Yes!" I fist-pump the air like Ali after a knockout.

My celebration is cut short by a knock at the door. Room service, I assume. Grabbing the remote, I turn down the volume. The last thing I need is the staff overhearing this circus from my suite.

"Here's your breakfast, Ms. Collins," the young waiter says with a polite smile. "Would you like me to set it up?"

"No, I've got it," I reply, wheeling the cart inside and shutting the door behind it. No tip, no small talk—I don't have the time or energy.

I glance at the spread, but my appetite is gone. Instead, I rush to the closet and throw on a Fendi short set with matching sneakers. Pulling my hair into a messy bun, I toss my phone into my bag and head for the door. The muffled sounds of Agent Cochran rattling off Raul's aliases fade as I leave, but her words echo in my mind.

Jason Montgomery. The man I thought I loved. The man who turned my life upside down.

19

The elevator jerks to a stop. When the doors slide open, I spot a man arguing with the front desk clerk. His voice is low but heated, his frustration apparent. As I step over the threshold, a security guard starts toward me. I pull my Fendi shades from my purse and slide them over my eyes. I didn't hear anything. I didn't see anything. I'm on a mission.

"Mickey! Mick!"

The shout paralyzes me for a moment.

I turn, the voice dragging me out of my tunnel vision. It's the man from the desk, now flanked by two security guards gripping his arms.

"Mickey, it's me."

I squint, taking a few steps closer. Recognition hits like a punch to the gut.

"It's me, Mick. It's Booker," he says, his tone softer now, almost pleading.

Damn. I didn't see it right away, but now that I do, it's impossible to miss. He still looks good—too damn good—and I hate it. The Tom Ford Soleil Blanc radiates from him like a spell, pulling me in against my will. The chain-stitched jeans, Supreme black tee, and effortless confidence scream street king. He's setting off all my senses, and I'm thrown.

I'm not ready for this.

"Miss Collins, do you know this gentleman?" Steven, the hotel manager, asks, his tone measured.

I take a deep breath, steadying myself. "Yes, Steven. Unfortunately, I do." Smacking my lips, I slide my shades back on and continue walking.

Booker pulls free of the guards and follows me.

"Damn, it's like that?" he asks, catching up easily.

"Where the hell is my car?" I snap, directing my frustration at the valet instead of him. "I called down here ten minutes ago!"

"Mick—"

"What, Booker? What?" I spin to face him, arms folded, already exhausted. This is too much. I can't deal with him, not here, not now.

He steps back, hands raised in surrender. I sigh heavily, resigned. It looks like being back in this city means facing all my demons, whether I'm ready or not.

"How'd you find me?" I ask.

"What do you mean?" He shrugs, casual. "The streets have been buzzing since word got out you were back. Everybody knows the queen's home."

"No, Booker. How did you find me here?" I gesture to the hotel, my patience fraying.

"Oh, that." He grins like it's no big deal. "Carmen. I knew she'd know where you were staying."

Of course. I should've known.

"Why are you here?" I ask, voice low. "Did you think you could just show up and everything would go back to the way it was? I don't understand what this is about."

Booker's smile fades. "Listen, Mick. I know we left things bad, but when I saw the news and heard you were back, I thought maybe... I don't know. Maybe you'd let me be there for you now."

I sigh again, the weight of it all pressing down on me. He's not wrong. I probably do need him. But my emotions are a mess, and I can't do this right now.

"Drinks later?" I ask, my tone softer.

His eyes light up with hope. "Yeah, I could go for a drink. Why later, though? Why not now?"

"I'm on my way to Yorkville." The valet finally pulls up with my car as the admission escapes my lips. "Don't bother holding your hand out – you're not getting shit." I snatch the keys from the attendant and shoot him a piercing glare.

Booker doesn't miss a beat. As soon as I climb into the driver's seat, he hops into the passenger side, closing the door before I can stop him.

"Yorkville, huh?" he says, leaning back as the engine roars to life.

I aim a scowl. "Say one word, and you're walking."

He smirks but says nothing. I crank up the stereo, letting the music fill the silence. As I press the gas and pull out onto the street, the city races by in a whirl of light and sound, stirring something familiar deep inside me.

The more things change, the more they stay the same.

20

"Do you know why we have you here?"

On the outside, I was solid—unflinching—but inside, my heart raced, my mind spiraling through a million possibilities.

This was my first time in an interrogation room.

From the moment they dragged me out of the Echelon to the two hours I'd spent in this cramped space, I hadn't said a word. You'd think they'd have gotten the hint by now.

I took a slow, deep breath, steadying myself. I'd learned how to put on for the streets—how to play the part of the untouchable bad bitch—but handcuffs and the alphabet police? That wasn't the move. Not for me.

If this was the game, I had to play by its rules.

One of the detectives stood, slipping his hands into his pockets. Just as he opened his mouth to speak, the door knocked and swung open.

And in walked a face I never thought I'd see again: Donovan.

The street cop who, in a roundabout way, had led me to Hakeem in the first place.

"Detectives, do you mind giving me a moment alone with Ms. Collins?" His voice was deep, commanding.

Although they were DEA and he was just a NYPD street cop, he was very authoritative as though they worked for him and that his question was rhetorical.

The agents glanced at each other, annoyed but silent. Without a word, they gathered their folders and left.

Once the door closed, Donovan sat across from me, flashing a familiar smile.

"So, here we are again."

The tension in my shoulders eased, and I exhaled for what felt like the first time in hours.

"How are you, Mickey?" he asked, leaning back and crossing his arms.

"I'm fine," I snapped, keeping my guard up.

"You look… different than when I met you a few weeks ago," he said, his voice steady but probing.

"Well, when life gives you lemons…" I met his gaze, catching the warmth in his blue eyes.

"Do you trust me?" he asked, his tone serious.

"I don't even know you."

There's another knock at the door and it opens slowly.

"Just go with it." Donovan whispers as the door opens completely.

"Good afternoon, Mikayla. I'm Rachel Evans with Child Protective Services. I'll be your caseworker."

Here we go. I rolled my eyes instinctively.

Rachel smiled, standing next to Donovan. "When Officer Donovan heard about your father's arrest, he came to our office. He spoke very highly of you—said you're an honor roll student with a good head on your shoulders."

My stomach churned. Where was this going?

"With everything you've been through," she continued, "we believe stability is critical to your success."

"Which is why," Donovan interrupted, standing and clapping his hands, "I'd like you to come stay with me and my family."

I blinked, stunned.

"You want me to stay with your white family?" I laughed bitterly. "Is that a joke?"

"Is it so hard to believe?" he asked, his tone calm but insistent. He sits back down and bends over the table and looks at me caringly.

I feel my cheeks flushing. I Look up at the social worker for some understanding. A part of me wanted her to say he was just joking and that I would be going to a group home. I could still handle my business on the streets and get my money easier that way. However, another part of me wanted his words to be true. I could let all this shit go. I feel like I could be safe, and I would like to know what that feels like.

"That's right Mikayla." Rachel takes a seat now as well. "All of the paperwork has been completed and filed. Mr. Donovan is now your legal guardian at least until your father's case is closed. You will now be released into his custody.

KITTEN HEELS

"You ready for this?" Donovan asked, parking his Honda Passport in front of his modest Fort Lee home.

I let out a long breath, the weight of the past few hours pressing on my chest. "Let's get this over with."

On the porch, a picture-perfect family stood waiting. His blonde-haired wife and twin kids looked like they'd stepped out of a mix between Home Improvement and Married with Children. I was going to stick out here like pepper on rice.

"Mickey, this is my wife, Susan, and our twins, Justin and Justina," Donovan said, his tone easy, like he hadn't just flipped my world inside out.

Susan smiled warmly, stepping forward. She had that Farrah Fawcett vibe—glamorous, wholesome, and just a little too polished. The twins, who looked about my age, stood behind her, radiating clueless white privilege. Their plastered grins were as awkward as mine as our eyes met.

"Mikayla, it's so nice to meet you," Susan gushed, throwing her arms around me before I could dodge. "Jacob has told me so much about you."

I stiffened in her embrace, glancing over at Donovan. What the hell had he told her? That I was some hood project they were taking in?

Susan pulled back, still beaming. "Now, don't be rude, children. Say hello to Mickey."

"Hi," the twins said in perfect unison, their grins still frozen in place.

"Hey," I muttered, shoving my hands in my pockets.

An awkward silence fell over us until Susan clapped her hands together. "Well, I'm sure you're exhausted. Let's get you inside and settled."

The house was... quaint. Modest. Everything seemed to have its place. It wasn't flashy or grand like the homes I'd gotten used to in my short stint hustling, but it felt warm. It felt like a home—something I wasn't sure I'd ever experienced.

I wandered into the living room, where family photos lined the walls. Trophies from the twins' various sports were displayed on every available surface. Moving into the kitchen, I found more pictures stuck to the refrigerator, illuminated by the soft glow of sunlight streaming through the windows.

"This one is from our Christmas in Hilton Head last year," Susan said, joining me and pointing to a framed photo. She radiated pride as she gestured to the picture. It showed them all bundled up in earmuffs and gloves, standing outside a hotel with a massive Christmas tree in the background. Everyone was smiling like life couldn't get any better.

"Let me show you your room," Justina chimed in, grabbing my hand before I could say anything.

She led me down a hallway and stopped at the last door on the left. Throwing it open, she stepped inside and flopped onto the bed. "This is your room. Mine's right next door," she said, grinning. "I decorated it for you. What do you think?"

The room was an explosion of pink and fluff. It looked like a bottle of Pepto-Bismol had exploded. The bedspread was ruffled and there was a giant New Kids on the Block poster over the headboard.

"New Kids on the Block, huh?" I said, eyeing the poster with a raised eyebrow.

Justina lit up. "Aren't they awesome? I didn't know what kind of music you like, so I just put up one of my posters. You like it?"

"Sure." I flashed a tight, controlled smile, attempting to mask my true feelings. I wasn't sure how to act yet, and honestly, I didn't know how I was going to do this.

"Come on, let me show you the rest of the house!" she said, grabbing my hand and dragging me back into the hallway.

She gave me the full tour: the shared bathroom between our rooms, their parents' room at the end of the hallway – and finally Justin's room across the hall—which was painted red and covered in hip-hop posters. Justin barely acknowledged us when we barged in. He was sprawled on a beanbag, locked into a game of Grand Theft Auto, with Dr. Dre blasting in the background.

I liked his vibe. I had a feeling we'd get along.

"What do you want to do now?" Justina asked when the tour was over, her face bright with excitement.

"I'd really like to chill out," I said, pointing back to my room and bursting her bubble.

"Oh. Yeah. Sure. I get it," she said, her smile faltering. "I'll leave you to it."

Back in my new room—aka the Powerpuff Palace—I locked

the door and dropped my bag on the bed. Digging inside, I pulled out my phone. Thirty missed calls. Five voicemails. All from Booker.

I pressed play on the latest one.

"Yo, Mick. I'm sorry for peeling out on you like that Shorty, but I couldn't help you if we both got caught up. Listen, if you good and get this message, don't call me back. Just meet me at our spot. I'll be there every day at our time until you show. Oh, and get rid of your phone. Peace."

Our spot and our time? What the hell was he talking about?

Before I could figure it out, there was a knock at the door.

"Mick." Donovan's voice.

"Yeah?" I yelled, pulling the battery out of my phone and slipping it into my back pocket.

He didn't answer, but I could feel him waiting. I tossed the phone shell into my bag and opened the door. Sure enough, Donovan was standing there.

"It's time for supper," he said, his tone gentle but firm. "Come eat."

The dining table was set, and Susan brought out casserole dishes as the twins finished arranging plates and silverware. I slid into a chair, trying to disappear as everyone else took their seats.

The food… was not it. The chicken was bland, the mashed potatoes were chunky, and the broccoli tasted like nothing at all. I pushed the food around my plate, wondering if these people were trying to kill me.

"I need some air," I blurted, standing and heading for the door that led to the backyard.

Outside, I breathed deeply, letting the cool evening air fill my lungs. In the corner of the yard, I spotted a gazebo near the fence. I made my way over, pulling the phone battery from my pocket and hurling it over the fence before sinking onto the bench inside.

I'd barely been there a minute when I heard footsteps.

"Mind if I join you?" Donovan asked, his hands stuffed into his jean pockets.

"You're here now," I muttered, sitting up straighter.

"Mickey, I know this isn't easy," he began, his voice soft. "This is a big change, and it's happened fast. I just want you to know—you're not alone."

"What do you want from me?" My voice came out sharper than I intended, but I didn't care. "Why are you 'trying' to help me?"

Donovan sighed, sitting beside me. "Did you know I'm from West Harlem too? 149th. Sugar Hill."

That got my attention. I glanced at him, skeptical.

"I know the life, Mick. I've been there. And I see so much potential in you. You're going to do something special in this world—I can feel it."

I finally raised my head and looked over at him, my voice sharper than I intended. "I can't move schools, and I need to talk to my friends. There are going to be times when I'll have to go places, and I can't tell you where or why. If you can't handle that, take me back to ACS and let them drop me in a group home."

Donovan didn't flinch. "Look, Mickey, I get it. I know what's up—the streets are talking. But if I let you run back out there, I can't protect you."

"Oh, so now you're my protector?" I shot back, my arms folding defensively.

"Mickey." His tone softened, but his eyes locked on mine, steady and unyielding. "Do you want to make it through this?"

"Yes." The word escaped before I could think twice. I meant it.

"Then let me help you." He reached for my hand, gently pulling it away from my clenched fists. His touch was firm, steadying. "I know you're just trying to stack your bread, get out, and make something of yourself. I know. But there's a better way, a smarter way."

I yanked my hand back, slamming both palms against my thighs in frustration. "I'm doing what I have to do! You don't get it!"

"I do get it, Mickey." His voice cut through the air like a sword, but his expression remained calm. "I know what it's like to feel like the whole world's against you. Like there's only one way out, and it's through the grind. I was you once. I've been where you are."

I froze, caught off guard by the quiet conviction in his voice.

"Let me tell you something." He leaned in, his voice low, deliberate. "I see you. You're sharp, resourceful, and determined.

You've got the kind of potential that most people would kill for. But if you keep running the way you're running, it's only a matter of time before you burn out—or worse."

The air between us grew still, heavy with unspoken truths. I glanced down, my anger cooling into something closer to exhaustion.

"There's a wrong way and a right way to do this," Donovan continued, his voice fixed but kind. "You're playing a game where the stakes are your life. Let me help you figure out the rules so you can win—without losing yourself."

I swallowed hard, his words pressing against the walls I'd built around myself. For a moment, I let myself believe him.

"Alright," I whispered, lifting my honey brown eyes to meet his icy blues. "I'll trust you."

He smiled, a flicker of relief crossing his face. He reached out and clasped my hand in his, sealing the unspoken pact. "Alright."

Letting go, he leaned back, his tone shifting back to business. "To start, you'll stay in school at Saint Mark's. You can keep in touch with your friends, but we need boundaries. No unplanned trips to 'unknown locations.' If you're the new Princess of the game, like they're saying, no one from the streets should know your face—or where you're going to be. Got it?"

"Got it," I replied, the words coming easier than I expected.

"Good," Donovan said, standing and stretching before turning to leave. "Whatever there is to handle, someone else needs to be handling it. Not you."

I watched him walk away, the heaviness of his words settling over me like a blanket. For the first time in a long time, I felt like maybe—just maybe—there was a way out.

21

Out of all the days in my life, that day changed everything. It was the pivot point—the moment that turned me into the woman you see today. Donovan didn't just save me from the streets; he reshaped my understanding of the game. He taught me what I couldn't learn from being in it—how to step back, see the whole board, and move like a boss.

The first lesson came during a fundraiser. Donovan had insisted I attend, saying it was time I started understanding the world beyond the streets. The ballroom was packed with New York's elite, a sea of black tuxedos and glittering gowns. I was dressed in a custom emerald green cocktail dress that shimmered under the chandeliers. It was a gift from Donovan, chosen specifically to command attention without crossing the line into excess.

"Keep your head high," Donovan murmured, his hand resting lightly on my shoulder as he guided me through the crowd. "First rule: You're never invisible. People are watching, even when they're pretending not to."

I nodded, eager to absorb every word. Donovan was dressed

in a sharp navy suit, his presence commanding without being overbearing. He nodded to someone across the room, his expression calm but calculating.

"That's Councilman Turner," he said, his voice low. "He's got a thing for young, sharp minds. Go introduce yourself. Ask about his latest bill."

I hesitated, my heart pounding. "What if I screw it up?"

Donovan's hand squeezed my shoulder gently. "You won't. Just listen. People like Turner love to hear themselves talk. Smile, nod, and act interested. That's all it takes."

Taking a deep breath, I approached the councilman. I was nervous, but Donovan's confidence in me gave me strength. Turner lit up at my questions, launching into a long-winded explanation about infrastructure improvements. By the time I returned to Donovan's side, the councilman had promised to introduce me to three of his "influential" friends.

"Not bad," Donovan said, a rare smile tugging at his lips. "You didn't just get a conversation; you got access. That's the second rule: Always leave with more than you came for."

Later, Donovan pulled me aside into a quieter corner of the ballroom. "Look around," he said, motioning toward the crowd. "What do you see?"

I scanned the room. "Power?"

"No," he said, shaking his head. "You see people who think they're powerful. Real power doesn't boast, Mickey. It moves in silence. It's the woman over there,"—he nodded toward an unassuming older woman standing near the bar—"who owns

KITTEN HEELS

half the real estate in Manhattan. Or the man by the window who runs a lobbying firm that can kill a bill before it's even drafted. Those are the people you watch."

His words stuck with me, reshaping the way I saw every room I walked into from that day forward.

A few weeks later, Donovan took me to a stock trading floor. The chaos was overwhelming—phones ringing, people shouting, screens flashing numbers faster than my eyes could track. But Donovan was calm, his presence grounding.

"This," he said, gesturing to the floor, "is where futures are bought and sold. Not just stocks, but ideas, power, influence. You don't need to understand every number on the board; you just need to know who controls them."

He introduced me to a trader named Carl, a wiry man with a sharp tongue and sharper instincts. "Carl's going to teach you the basics," Donovan said. "Not because I expect you to trade, but because I want you to understand the language. If you can speak their language, you can speak to anyone."

Carl didn't go easy on me. He threw terms like "short selling" and "options" at me until my head spun, but Donovan's voice was always in the back of my mind: "Stay sharp. Stay curious." By the end of the week, I could hold my own in a conversation about the market—a skill that would prove invaluable in the years to come.

As my influence grew, so did his—from beat cop to Chief of Police to the Mayor of New York.

But it wasn't just Donovan's lessons that shaped me. Booker

had been there, too, in those early years, pushing me in ways Donovan couldn't. While Donovan showed me the power of patience and strategy, Booker taught me how to trust my instincts—how to think on my feet when the rules broke down. He kept me sharp, made sure I knew how to handle myself when the stakes were high and the clock was ticking.

My attention is shifted to the passenger seat, where Booker is turning the radio, burning a hole in my face with those almond-shaped eyes. That same intensity—like he could see through me—hadn't dulled in all these years. I had to admit: Booker was just as vital to my growth as Donovan. I wouldn't have made it through without him.

The memory of our "spot" and "time" flashes through my mind—the breakfast joint where we had eaten that morning. It had been obvious in hindsight; it was the only spot we had went together but that point. I gave him the new play the next day, with one condition: he and Donovan had to work together. I needed them both.

The memories tugged at me as I pulled up to the gate. A smile crept across my face. The gate creaks open without a word from the intercom. I take a deep breath, preparing myself.

"Oh! We seeing the homie?!" Booker grins, his tone light but full of meaning.

"You guys been keeping in touch?" I ask, curious.

"No doubt." He looks at me as though I should know better.

Mayor Jacob Donovan waited on the third-to-last step of the grand colonial-style home. His calm demeanor was a masterclass in control, but as I stepped out of the car, I saw the glint of something deeper in his eyes.

Booker hopped out first, clasping Donovan's hand in an easy, familiar grip. Before I could grab my purse, a middle-aged staffer approached and opened my door.

"Allow me, ma'am," he said, offering a steady hand.

"Thank you." I placed my hand in his and stepped out, smoothing my outfit as I circled to face Donovan.

We stood there, locked in an unspoken exchange. His piercing eyes took me in, reading the years written in my posture, my presence, the subtle changes in my face.

Finally, he pulled me into a firm embrace. The hug lingered, warm and steady, before he pulled back to hold me at arm's length.

"Michael, please take Miss Collins' vehicle around back," Donovan said to the staffer without breaking eye contact.

Turning to Booker and me, he moved toward the house. "Come. We have a lot to discuss."

Inside, the foyer gleamed with polished wood and marble. A black-and-white rose etched into the floor created the illusion of stepping into a living bloom. To the right, the living room opened up with plush seating and ornate decor. To the left, a winding staircase curved toward the second floor.

Donovan led us past the dining room and into his study. Dark wood paneling and rich leather furniture gave the space a warm, powerful presence. He turned to a maid standing nearby.

"Hold all my calls. No interruptions," he instructed, then closed the door with a decisive click. Turning back to us, he clapped his hands together, a wide grin spreading across his face.

"Anyone want a drink?" he asked, already moving toward the bar in the corner.

"Yes," Booker and I said in unison.

I took a seat on the sofa, the marble fireplace casting a soft glow against the room's polished surfaces.

"How are Susan and the twins?" I asked, breaking the silence.

Donovan froze mid-pour, the question hitting him like a slap to the face, leaving him momentarily speechless.

"Justin and Justina are grown now. Justina's married with three kids and works as a public defender for the city. Justin runs In the Mix Records. He's doing well." A shadow crossed his face before he added, "And Susan and I… split five years ago."

My gaze dropped to the fireplace, guilt curling in my stomach. Life had gotten away from me, and I hadn't kept in touch like I should have.

"I'm sorry to hear that," I offer softly as he hands me a glass of brandy.

"That's life," he says simply, taking a seat across from me.

Booker joins him, and suddenly I feel like I'm in an intervention. I stood, restless, and wandered to the window overlooking the grounds. The gardeners moved with practiced precision, keeping the property pristine. My eyes lingered on the etchings in the window frame, carved by the many who had passed through this house over the years.

"So, you both know what's going on?" I asked, my back to them.

Donovan's voice was steady as he began. "Jason Montgomery was born in El Fanguito, Puerto Rico. His father was killed in a gang war when he was three. Not long after, his mother moved him to Miami. By sixteen, he'd been arrested seven times—for theft, drug paraphernalia, the usual."

He walked closer, refilling his glass as he continued. "By eighteen, he'd built a name for himself in the criminal underworld. Using his first alias, Darin Taylor, he moved to Georgia and established Turnabout Holdings, LLC. What followed was one of the largest international fraud syndicates since the eighties. He became one of the most wanted con artists in the world."

I turned, bitterness curling my lip. "Con artist," I say, spitting the words, moving bitterly back to the sofa and smacking back down onto it. I finished my drink in one swallow, holding the glass up for a refill.

"Let me get that," Booker offers, taking my glass.

"Do we know where to find him?" I asked, pushing myself up and making my way over to them.

Donovan's eyes met mine. "And what will you do when you find him?"

"That's none of your concern, Mr. Mayor," I snapped,

grabbing my glass mid-pour, spilling liquor across the bar.

"Now, wait a minute." His voice dropped, cool but cutting. "I don't recall doing anything to wrong you, Mikayla. If I missed a memo, let me know."

He was right, of course. I was lashing out at the wrong person. The anger bubbling inside wasn't for him—or even for Booker. It was for me. I'd let myself be played. I'd been too blinded to see the truth about Raul.

"You're right," I admitted, pacing. "You're so fucking right. I should've seen it. You taught me better than this. Both of you did."

I stopped and faced them, staring at the two men who molded me my composure cracks. Donovan stepped forward, pulling me into another firm embrace.

"Now, now," he murmured, soothing me. He guided me to a nearby chair and crouched before me, his eyes searching mine. "You've worked hard to get where you are, Mickey. Don't let this undo you. But you have to be smart—there's no room for mistakes."

Booker spoke up, his tone deliberate. "Turns out this cat used to fly an escort out to a house in Havana. We're thinking that's where he's holed up."

"No extradition treaty," Donovan added, his expression grim.

My wheels turn. "Cuba, huh?"

Booker nodded, meeting my gaze. He knew where this was going.

"So how do we play this?" I asked, leaning in. My voice was calm, my eyes biting.

This felt like old times.

22

Jason Montgomery had built an empire on deception, and Havana was his sanctuary—a place where power met paradise, cloaked in the guise of legitimacy. The compound stood on the outskirts of the city, surrounded by dense tropical foliage and perched high on a bluff that overlooked the shimmering blue of the Straits of Florida. From this vantage point, Montgomery could see everything and everyone coming his way.

The compound itself was a marvel of modern design. High stone walls lined with surveillance cameras encased the property. The main house, a sprawling, low-slung villa with clean, angular lines, was painted a muted cream that blended into the landscape. Behind it, a series of smaller outbuildings housed everything from guest accommodations to an operations center bristling with technology. There was even a helipad, its stark black surface a reminder of just how quickly Montgomery could vanish if the need arose.

Inside the main villa, Montgomery's world came into focus. The foyer was understated but elegant, its polished concrete floors leading into a series of open, airy rooms filled with carefully curated art and furniture. The walls were lined with screens displaying live feeds from security cameras, maps of global markets, and news updates. Montgomery liked to stay informed—an understatement if ever there was one.

Seated behind a massive glass desk in his study, Montgomery exuded a calm, calculating air. He was in his mid-forties but carried himself like a man much older. His tailored linen shirt was open at the collar, revealing just a hint of a gold chain. His face was sharp and angular, his eyes cold and piercing. He was the kind of man who never raised his voice but could make the hair on the back of your neck stand up with a single look.

"Where are we with the shipment?" he asked, his voice smooth and unhurried. He leaned back in his chair, fingers steepled.

Across the desk, Ricardo, his second-in-command, shifted uncomfortably. "The shipment is en route from Panama. It should arrive within 48 hours."

Montgomery's gaze sharpened. "Should?"

Ricardo cleared his throat. "There was… a delay at the port. Customs flagged one of the containers. We had to reroute."

"And what are you doing to ensure this doesn't happen again?" Montgomery asked, his tone icy.

Ricardo fumbled for an answer, but Montgomery waved him off with a dismissive hand. "I don't pay you to make excuses, Ricardo. Fix it."

As Ricardo retreated, Montgomery's attention shifted to

the screens on the wall. One in particular displayed a live feed of the compound's perimeter. Guards patrolled in pairs, their movements precise and coordinated. Each guard carried an automatic weapon, and Montgomery had personally ensured they were all former military—men who knew how to follow orders without question.

Montgomery's network was vast and intricate, spanning everything from offshore accounts to shell companies that masked his operations. In Havana, he operated with impunity, protected by a combination of bribes, blackmail, and the island's lack of an extradition treaty with the United States.

But Montgomery wasn't one to rest on his laurels. He knew better than anyone that empires built on deception were fragile. That's why he maintained a level of paranoia that bordered on obsession. His phone calls were encrypted, his meetings carefully staged. Even his personal chef underwent rigorous security checks.

As the day gave way to evening, Montgomery stepped out onto the villa's expansive terrace. Below, the lights of Havana twinkled like a thousand tiny stars, their glow reflecting off the water. A warm breeze rustled the palm trees, carrying with it the distant sound of music and laughter from the city. It was beautiful, yes, but Montgomery saw the world in shades of risk and reward, not sentiment.

His phone buzzed, breaking the moment. He glanced at the screen, his expression darkening as he answered. "What is it?"

The voice on the other end was curt and to the point. "We've picked up chatter. Someone's asking questions about you. A woman. She's connected."

Montgomery's grip on the phone tightened. "Mickey Collins."

There was a pause. "You think she'll come here?"

A slow smile spread across Montgomery's face, but there was a brief flare of something else in his eyes—an emotion he thought he'd buried. Mickey wasn't just another name on a list to him. She had started out as a mark, yes, but she'd become something else entirely. He'd underestimated her once, and in doing so, he'd let himself get too close. When the feds closed in on him in Atlanta, he hadn't just been relieved to escape—he'd been happy. Happy to leave the temptation of her behind, happy for an excuse to sever a bond that was becoming dangerous.

And now, she was looking for him.

"If she's as smart as they say, she will," Montgomery said, his smile returning, harder this time. "And when she does, we'll be ready."

He ended the call and turned back toward the villa. The lights flickered briefly, a reminder that even in a fortress, there were vulnerabilities. But Montgomery thrived on the challenge. To him, risk wasn't something to be avoided; it was something to be managed, controlled, and, when necessary, eliminated.

He poured himself a glass of rum from a crystal decanter and raised it in a silent toast to the darkness. "Come on, Mickey," he murmured. "Let's see if you're as good as they say."

This man thought his fortress made him untouchable. But no matter how high the walls or how many cameras he had, I'd find my way in. I had to - because taking him down wasn't just about business. It was personal.

23

The sun dipped low as we worked in the basement of the mayoral home, the golden light clashing with the grim reality of the moment. Papers, maps, and dossiers; everything that the three of us were able to gather independently lay scattered across the table, every detail scrutinized and cross-checked. The air was thick with unspoken thoughts, each of us weighing our words carefully. There was no room for mistakes now.

Donovan sat at the head of the table, flipping through a file with the casual efficiency of a man who'd seen it all. But I knew better. Behind his calm exterior, he was already calculating the risks, planning for every contingency. Years of navigating the game on both sides of the law had taught him the cost of a single misstep.

Across from him, Booker leaned back in his chair, arms crossed, tapping a slow rhythm on his bicep. His laid-back posture didn't fool me. His mind was always working, five steps ahead, waiting for the right moment to speak.

I tried to focus, but my thoughts drifted. Each passing

minute felt heavier. I gripped the edge of the table, grounding myself, but the faint buzz of adrenaline coursing through me only made it worse. Jason Montgomery. Raul Santiago. Whatever the hell his name was. My revenge was close, but every step toward it felt like pulling open an old wound.

"Alright, Mikayla." Donovan's voice broke the silence, sharp and steady. "We need to get in touch with Bird."

The name stopped me cold. My cousin. My sister in everything but blood. The woman I thought I'd find in Brooklyn, still connected to the shadows we'd left behind.

"Bird?" I repeated, frowning. "What does she have to do with this?"

"She's in Havana," Donovan replied, his tone matter-of-fact.

Havana. The word hit me like a punch. "Havana?" I stared at him, trying to process what he'd just said. "What's she doing there? Last I heard, she was in Brooklyn."

Booker leaned forward, his voice quieter but firm. "She married some ex-baseball player. Big name. They've been living large down there for a while now."

The revelation slammed into me. Bird. In Havana. Married. Living large. All this time, I'd been picturing her in a Brooklyn brownstone, still hustling on the edges of a gentrified neighborhood, while she'd gone and built a life I didn't even know about.

I thought back to the other day, standing on the stoop,

expecting Bird. I'd prepared myself for whatever version of my cousin would answer the door—whether she was thriving or barely surviving. But Bird hadn't been there. Instead, I found Love. Sober. Mended. A stranger. That moment had shattered something in me, and now Donovan was telling me Bird hadn't just left Brooklyn—she'd left it all.

My stomach twisted. "You're telling me Bird's in Havana, married and playing house, while I've been here thinking she's…" I trailed off, shaking my head.

Donovan nodded, unbothered by my tone. "Yes. And she's connected. If anyone can help us track down Montgomery without tipping him off, it's her."

"She's not the same Bird we used to run with," I said, crossing my arms. "She's out of the game. I'm not dragging her back into this."

"She's not out," Donovan said firmly. "She's just moved her hustle to a different playground. She still has ties to Havana's underworld, and she's in a position to open doors we can't. You know that as well as I do."

My hands tightened into fists. He wasn't wrong. Bird had always loved the hustle. Even as Tamika Acosta, wife of a retired pro baseball star, she wasn't the type to sit on the sidelines. But knowing she still had her hands in the game didn't make this easier.

"You think she'll help us?" I asked, doubt heavy in my voice.

Booker gave me a knowing look. "You're family, Mick. She

ain't gonna leave you hanging. You just gotta remind her where she came from."

"She didn't leave Brooklyn clean, did she?" I asked, my voice quieter.

"She didn't leave clean," Donovan confirmed. "That's why she's the key. She knows the game, and she knows Havana. This is her world now."

I felt the weight of it all pressing down on me. Bird wasn't just a contact. She was family. And asking her for help meant asking her to risk everything she'd built.

"Alright," I said finally, the words tasting bitter. "I'll make the call. But if she says no, we're back to square one."

Donovan's gaze locked onto mine. "We won't let it come to that. But if Bird's in, we move fast. No mistakes, Mikayla."

I glanced at the map spread across the table, Havana's maze of streets and alleys staring back at me. It was the perfect place for someone like Jason Montgomery to disappear. If Bird didn't help, we'd be walking blind.

Booker gave me a reassuring pat on the back as he got to his feet. "You got this."

I just nodded as they left the room, my mind racing.

The phone felt heavier than it should as I scrolled through my contacts. Bird and I had been inseparable back then, especially after everything with Stone. She'd gone to places when I needed to stay hidden, been my voice when my silence needed to be loud. We were bad bitches before that was a badge of honor.

But when Spelman offered me a way out, I took it, leaving Bird behind to find her own way.

Now I was about to call Bird, not knowing which version of her would answer.

I took a deep breath and dialed her number. The phone rang, each tone stretching out like a judgment.

Finally, the line clicked.

"Mickey?" Her voice was smooth, warm. Familiar, yet distant.

"Yeah, it's me," I said, my voice steadier than I felt. "I need your help."

A pause. Then, her tone sharpened. "I figured. I've seen the news. But last I checked, you weren't big on keeping in touch."

The words cut deep, but I bit back my frustration. "You haven't exactly been calling me either."

Another pause, heavy with unspoken truths.

"If you've seen the news, you know why I need to find this motherfucker, Bird. I don't have time to play around."

She let out a long sigh. "What do you need?"

"We got word Jason Montgomery's in Havana. I need a contact—someone who can help us track him without tipping him off."

Her breath caught on the other end, and I could feel the hesitation in her silence before she spoke. "And what are you going to do when you find him, Mick? You're not a suspect anymore. Why go this route?"

I hesitated, her question hitting me harder than I expected.

The truth was, I didn't know. I didn't have an answer—not for her, not for Donovan, not even for myself.

A part of me wanted to ask him why. Why me? Why did he choose me, play with my heart, and turn my life upside down? I wanted to look him in the eye and demand to know what I'd done to deserve this. Was it all some elaborate game to him? Was there ever a moment when he cared, or was I just another mark, another step in his con?

But then there was the darker part of me, the one that was louder, harder to ignore. That part didn't want answers. It wanted revenge. I wanted to make him hurt in ways he couldn't even imagine. I wanted to strip away everything he thought made him untouchable, break him the way he'd broken me, and leave him with nothing.

The conflict churned inside me like a storm. One moment I craved closure, the next I was consumed by rage. Both parts of me felt justified, but neither offered a clear path forward.

"I don't know yet." I admitted finally.

Bird let out a long, deliberate sigh on the other end. The silence that followed was heavy, stretching out between us like an ocean.

She was quiet for a long moment. Then, finally: "Fine. I'll make some calls. But Mick, don't pull me too deep into this. I've worked hard to get where I am. I'm not about to lose it."

"You won't," I promised, even as guilt gnawed at me. "Just get me the contact. I'll handle the rest."

"Be careful," she warned. "The game's different now, and Havana isn't your turf."

The line clicked, leaving me in the silence of the room. Bird had agreed, but it wasn't just her help I'd gotten—it was a door back into the life we both tried to leave.

Now, it was up to me to make it count.

24

The morning air in New York felt heavier, as if the city itself were holding its breath. I stood in front of the penthouse window, staring at the skyline that stretched across Brooklyn and Manhattan. But it wasn't the city I saw—it was my own reflection in the glass, staring back at me, questioning me. The weight of what I was about to do pressed against my chest, suffocating.

Cuba. Havana. A place I thought I'd never return to. The last time I was there, it almost destroyed me. Now it was calling me back, the ghosts of my past clawing their way into my present. I gripped the windowsill tighter, feeling the knot in my stomach tighten.

"You lookin' at the city like it's about to disappear," Booker's voice cut through the stillness, smooth but edged with something unspoken.

I turned to see him leaning in the doorway, arms crossed, those deep brown eyes watching me like they always did—seeing more than I wanted him to. He'd always been able to read me, even when I wanted to stay hidden.

"I'm just thinking about Havana," I admitted, my voice softer than I intended. "It didn't end well the last time. Not for me, not for anyone involved."

Booker raised an eyebrow, his expression tightening. "Yeah, well, nothing ever ends clean. You know that better than anyone."

He was right. Messy endings were part of the life we chose—or maybe the life that chose us. But Havana wasn't just a messy ending; it carried a weight of personal loss. The last time I was there, I'd let myself believe in something better. I'd let myself trust someone. I glanced at Booker, the memory of his betrayal slamming into me like a wave.

That trip had been the reason I chose Spelman over NYU. The reason I ran.

The sound of polished shoes against hardwood drew my attention, and Donovan strode into the room, every inch the powerful politician he'd become. His tailored suit was sharp as a blade, his expression sharper. He carried himself with the kind of control that came from years of bearing impossible burdens.

"Alright," he began, his tone calm but charged with purpose. "Before we move forward, let me be clear. I'll be handling this discreetly," he said with a quiet authority. "I've got people on the inside, and I've been laying groundwork since I was elected in case of situations like this. I'll be able to disappear for a couple of days, keep the appearance of being in a meeting, and avoid any public attention. No one outside this room knows what's really happening, and I intend to keep it that way."

I raised an eyebrow, impressed. "You've got this all figured out, huh?"

Donovan gave a small, calculated smile. "I didn't get this far by leaving loose ends, Mikayla. Neither should you."

Booker snorted, his usual cocky grin slipping into place. "Mayor by day, covert operator by night. You might be more gangster than I am, Donovan."

Donovan didn't flinch. "Let's focus. "Booker, you've got contacts in Miami. Secure a safe house. I'll be working remotely from there while you guys are in Cuba. Mikayla…" His gaze shifted to me. "You're our wildcard. Use your charm."

I raised an eyebrow. "Charm? What exactly are you asking me to do?"

Donovan smiled, but it wasn't the kind of smile that reached his eyes. "Get us what we need. You know how to handle people."

I didn't ask for clarification. I knew what he meant. I'd spent years playing my angles, using every weapon in my arsenal—my connections, my presence, even my body when it came to it. But this time? This time I wasn't anyone's pawn.

"I'll get what we need," I said, the coldness in my voice surprising even me. "But let's get one thing straight, Donovan. I'm calling the shots."

Donovan studied me for a moment, his eyes narrowing slightly. Then, to my surprise, he nodded. "Fine," he said simply. "Two hours. Be ready."

The hum of the jet was steady, but my thoughts were anything but. As the Caribbean waters stretched endlessly below us, I found no solace in the serene view. Memories of Havana coiled around my mind, choking out the present. It wasn't just the place that haunted me—it was who I was there, what I'd lost, and who I'd lost it to.

Booker.

The last time I trusted someone to stand beside me without reservation, it was him. He'd been the only one who looked at me like I wasn't just a tool to be used or a player in someone else's game. Back then, I thought we could have it all. I thought he was my partner, my escape. But he left me. And in leaving, he shattered me in ways I never allowed myself to fully acknowledge.

His betrayal wasn't loud or violent—it was quiet, like a crack in the foundation that split everything apart. He hadn't just walked away; he'd walked away from us. He'd walked away from the plans we whispered under the stars, the future we'd started to build. After that, I'd spent years rebuilding myself—brick by brick, wall by wall—so no one could ever hurt me like that again.

And now? Here I was, working with him to chase down another man who had betrayed me. Another man who had promised partnership but turned it into ruin. The irony wasn't lost on me, and neither was the bitterness.

The first time Booker told me he loved me, it was my fifteenth birthday.

We were sitting on the hood of his BMW 7 Series, the city

lights stretching out before us from the rooftop of a parking garage. It was the first time in years I felt like someone saw me—not Mickey Collins, Stone's heir, the girl clawing her way through the game—but just me.

"Mick, I know we've talked about our future plans here and there, but now that Stone's in the pin and you've solidified your status in this game, do you still ever think about… more?" he asked, his voice uncharacteristically soft.

I laughed, leaning back on the windshield. "In what way?"

"More than…" He paused, glancing at me before finishing, "More than this." He stretches his arms out as if taking the whole city in his grasp.

I sat up, examining his face. Booker never showed vulnerability, not like this. "Where's this coming from?"

He shrugged, but there was something in his eyes, something that made my chest tighten. "I just been thinkin'. You're the smartest person I know. Toughest, too. You could do anything, Mick. Be anything."

"Book, what are you talking about?" I asked, my voice quieter now seeing a look in his eyes that confirmed that he was feeling for me what I had been feeling for him ever since our night in Times Square.

He exhaled, like he was about to jump off a cliff. "I'm saying I want more. I want… you."

The words hung in the air, heavy and unspoken until now. My breath caught, my heart pounding so loud I thought he could hear it.

KITTEN HEELS

"You mean that?" I asked, my voice barely above a whisper.

"Yeah," he said, his eyes locking onto mine. "I do."

And that was it. From that night on, it was me and Booker. The prince and princess of the streets, untouchable together. For two years, we built our empire side by side. He was the only person who ever saw me for who I really was, not just what I could do for him. We were in love—real love, the kind that makes you feel invincible. Until Havana.

The cantina was buzzing with tension as Señor Valdés left, his linen suit billowing as he stepped into the humid Havana night. The deal was done. Booker and I had secured a new supply line that would take our operation to the next level.

"You killed it," I said, nudging Booker as we walked back to the car. "Did you see his face when I shut down his counteroffer? Priceless."

Booker chuckled, sliding an arm around my shoulders. "That's my girl. Always keepin' them on their toes."

But something felt off. Booker was quieter than usual, his laugh lacking its usual warmth.

"What's on your mind?" I asked as we reached the car.

"Nothing," he said, brushing me off. "Let's just get back to the hotel."

Back at the suite, I kicked off my heels and collapsed onto the bed, relishing the cool air from the ceiling fan. Booker stood by the window, staring out at the city lights.

"You've been acting weird since the meeting," I said, sitting up. "What's going on?"

Booker turned, his face shadowed in the dim light. "I gotta step out for a bit."

"Step out? It's late," I said, frowning. "What's so important it can't wait?"

He avoided my gaze, grabbing his jacket. "Just some business I gotta handle. I'll be back."

Before I could argue, he was out the door.

I waited for hours, pacing the room and checking my phone, but there was no word from Booker. The unease in my chest grew heavier with every passing minute. When the door finally opened, I spun around, ready to demand answers.

"Where the hell have you been?" I snapped.

Booker looked... different. His shirt was wrinkled, his jaw tight, and there was something in his eyes I didn't recognize.

"Out," he said shortly, shrugging off his jacket.

"Out? That's all you've got? We're supposed to be in this together, and you're running off to God knows where?"

"Mick, don't start," he said, his voice low but laced with warning.

"Don't start?" I shot back, my anger boiling over. "You disappear without a word, come back looking like you've been through hell, and you don't even have the decency to explain yourself?"

Booker's jaw clenched, and he ran a hand over his face. "You don't get it, Mick."

"Then help me get it," I said, stepping closer. "What the hell is going on with you?"

He turned away, his hands gripping the edge of the dresser. "This life ain't for you."

I froze, his words slicing through me. "What are you talking about? We've been building this together. You can't just decide—"

"I can," he said, spinning around to face me. His voice cracked with something raw. "And I am. You need to get out, Mick. Go to school, live your life. You've got a future, and I'm not gonna let this life take it from you."

My heart pounded as I searched his face. "This isn't about me. This is about you. You're scared."

"Damn right I'm scared," he said, his voice rising. "You think Valdés is gonna let us play this game without a cost? These people don't play by our rules, Mick. They don't stop at threats. They'll come for you if they think it'll hurt me. And I can't… I can't let that happen."

Tears burned in my eyes, but I refused to let them fall. "So your solution is to push me away? To leave me behind?"

Booker's silence was answer enough.

"You're a coward," I whispered, my voice trembling.

He flinched, but he didn't argue. "I'm doin' this for you, Mick. Whether you believe it or not."

I stood there, frozen, as he grabbed his bag and walked out the door. I waited for him to turn around, to say something—anything—but he didn't.

He was gone.

The memory hit me like a wave, dragging me under. I

leaned my head back against the seat, closing my eyes as the jet hummed around me. The memory of that rooftop felt distant now, like it belonged to someone else. Booker had been the only person I ever let in completely, and when he left, he took something with him I hadn't gotten back.

But now? Sitting here, with his presence just a row away, I felt something shift. The walls I'd built so carefully over the years didn't feel as solid anymore. They felt... fragile. And I wasn't sure if that was a good thing or a warning.

When the betrayal came, it felt just as quiet as the love had been. It was a whispered goodbye wrapped in the lie of protection. He thought walking away was saving me. He didn't understand it was breaking me.

And yet, here we were. Not the same kids on the hood of that BMW, but not entirely different either.

The jet dipped slightly, signaling our descent, and I opened my eyes, turning toward him. Booker glanced my way, his expression unreadable, but there was something in his eyes that took my breath.

I hadn't seen Booker since that night, hadn't heard from him, either. I never knew where he went or why he'd really left, but his words stayed with me, festering like an open wound.

"Doin' this for you."

I clenched my fists, staring out at the shimmering city below. It was the same line I'd been telling myself for years—that leaving Havana, leaving the life, had been for the best. But now? Now I wasn't so sure.

Booker's voice snapped me out of my head. "You good?"

"I'm fine," I said, the lie falling easily from my lips.

He didn't push, but the silence between us felt heavier than the cabin air. I knew he was still watching me, but I didn't care. I couldn't let him see how much of the past still haunted me. Not now. Not when everything depended on me keeping my head in the game.

As the jet bounces to a stop, I made myself a promise: I wouldn't let this city break me again. I wouldn't let Booker—or anyone—see me weak. Jason Montgomery would answer for what he'd done, and I would leave this place with my dignity intact.

This wasn't just about revenge. It was about reclaiming my power.

25

The humid heat of Havana wrapped around me the second I stepped off the plane, thick and suffocating. It smelled the same—salt from the ocean, tobacco hanging heavy in the air, and the faint metallic tang of the city's unrest. The memories it dredged up came unbidden, each one scratching at the edges of my focus.

I adjusted my sunglasses, tilting my head toward Booker as we crossed the tarmac to the waiting car. He hadn't said much since Miami, not to me, anyway. Fine by me. There was enough between us already—words would only complicate things further.

"Be sharp, Mikayla," Donovan had said before we left Miami. "This isn't just about getting in and out. I'll be here to coordinate, but Havana's yours. Don't let it own you."

He didn't have to tell me twice.

From the air-conditioned safety of the car, Havana's streets felt like a different world. The city buzzed with life, colorful vintage cars navigating cobblestone streets, locals chatting on stoops, and music spilling from every corner. But beneath the vibrant façade, I felt it—danger humming just out of reach.

Booker sat silently next to me, his eyes fixed on the scenery as if searching for something. Or maybe someone.

"You gonna keep brooding the whole time, or are you gonna say something useful?" I asked, breaking the silence.

He didn't look at me, just smirked faintly. "Don't need to say much. You're already wound tight."

I scoffed, leaning back against the seat. "Not as tight as you think."

The driver pulled up in front of the safe house—a nondescript building in Vedado with whitewashed walls and a faint smell of damp concrete. Bird's contact had made arrangements for us to stay here while we worked the ground in Havana. Donovan had insisted on splitting up, setting himself up in Miami to manage the operation remotely.

"You've got Bird's people on the ground in Cuba," Donovan had said back in Miami, leaning over the table where our plans were laid out. "I'll handle things from here—secure the escape route, arrange the jet. Once you have the target, I'll be ready to move you out. No delays."

"You trust Bird's contact?" Booker had asked, his tone skeptical.

"I trust Mikayla to figure that out," Donovan replied, his eyes flicking to me. "And I trust you to back her up."

Booker's nod was all we got, his expression fixed in a quiet mask, and I didn't bothered to push.

Inside the safe house, the air was cool but stifling in its own way. Booker claimed the far bedroom without a word, leaving me to pace the small living area.

The silence didn't last long.

My phone buzzed with a message from Donovan. "Contact confirmed. Meeting is set for tonight. Stay sharp."

It was a simple directive, but the weight of it pressed down on me. Bird's contact was the key to finding Montgomery, but this city wasn't the same Havana I'd left years ago. And I wasn't the same, either.

"You got something?" Booker asked, reemerging from the bedroom.

"Donovan set up the meeting," I said, slipping my phone into my pocket. "Bar in Old Havana. We leave in an hour."

Booker leaned against the doorframe. "You think this guy's legit?"

I shrugged. "Bird wouldn't steer me wrong."

"She wouldn't steer you wrong," he repeated, his tone tense.

I ignored the implication. Bird and I might have drifted, but trust wasn't something I questioned when it came to her. Not yet, anyway.

The bar was a hole-in-the-wall, its dim lighting and peeling paint a stark contrast to the lively music spilling into the street. Inside, the air was thick with cigar smoke and the chatter of locals.

I scanned the room, spotting our man near the back—a wiry figure nursing a glass of rum, his sharp eyes watching the door.

"That him?" Booker asked, his voice low.

"That's him," I replied, making my way over.

The man's gaze locked to me as I approached, his expression neutral but alert.

"You must be Mickey," he said in accented English. "Bird told me to expect you."

"And you are?"

"Ramón," he said, extending a hand.

I shook it, noting the roughness of his palm. This wasn't a man who stayed out of the fray.

"You've got something for us?"

Ramón nodded, gesturing for us to follow. He led us out a back door and into an alley, the din of the bar fading behind us. He pulled out a folded map, spreading it on the hood of a rusted car.

"Montgomery's got a compound outside the city," he said, pointing to a marked location. "Tight security. Armed guards, cameras, the works. But there's a way in—an old service road. It'll get you close without being seen."

"What's the risk?" Booker asked, his voice sharp.

"The risk," Ramón said with a wry smile, "is that if you're seen, you're dead."

I folded the map, slipping it into my bag. "We'll handle it."

Ramón nodded, lighting a cigarette. "Good luck. You're gonna need it."

The safe house was silent except for the faint hum of the ceiling fan as Booker and I sat across from each other at the small wooden table. The map Ramón had given us was spread out between us, its edges curling slightly from the humidity. Every inch of the layout was burned into my mind—Montgomery's compound, the service road, the potential blind spots in the guard patrols. It all felt dangerously thin.

Booker leaned back in his chair, his arms crossed, his eyes scanning the map like it held some hidden answer. He'd been quiet since we got back from the meeting, but that wasn't unusual. Booker had always been one to think before he spoke.

"You know this is a trap, right?" he said finally, his voice low but edged with humor.

"It's not a trap," I shot back, not looking up from the map.

"It's always a trap," he said, his smirk tugging at the corner of his lips. "People don't just hand over information for free. Ramón's either getting paid, or he's trying to stay alive by throwing us to the wolves."

I sighed, folding the edge of the map to crease it tighter. "Bird vouched for him. That's enough for me."

"Bird vouched for him, sure," Booker said, leaning forward, his elbows on the table. "But who's vouching for Bird these days? You haven't talked to her in years."

That hit a nerve, and he knew it. I glared at him, my fingers tightening on the map. "You think I don't know that? You think I don't know the risk?"

Booker's smirk faded, his gaze softening slightly. "Mick, I didn't mean it like that."

"Then how did you mean it?" I snapped.

Booker leaned back again, running a hand across his jaw.

For a moment, he looked like he wanted to say something, but instead, he just chuckled. "You're still the same, you know that? Always ready to bite someone's head off."

"Maybe I wouldn't be so quick to bite if people didn't keep giving me reasons," I shot back, turning my attention back to the map.

The silence between us stretched, heavy with the weight of things left unsaid.

"I missed this," Booker said quietly, almost to himself.

I froze, my eyes still on the map but no longer seeing it.

"This?" I asked, my voice laced with disbelief. "You missed sitting in some rundown safe house planning a mission that could get us both killed?"

Booker laughed softly, the sound warm but hollow. "I missed you, Mick. I missed… us."

The air between us shifted, the tension thickening. I didn't look at him, didn't dare meet his eyes.

"You don't get to say that," I said, my voice low and steady. "Not after what you did."

Booker sighed, leaning forward again, his elbows on the table. "Mick, I didn't—"

"Don't," I interrupted, finally looking up at him. My gaze locked onto his, hard and unyielding. "Don't try to explain it away. You left. You didn't just leave Havana—you left me."

Booker's posture tightened, the certainty he always wore slipping away in an instant. "I thought I was doing the right thing."

"For who?" I asked, my voice rising. "Because it sure as hell wasn't for me."

He didn't answer right away, his jaw tightening as he looked down at the map. "I thought I was protecting you," he said finally, his voice barely above a whisper.

"Protecting me?" I repeated, disbelief flooding my tone. "You broke me, Booker. You don't protect someone by breaking them."

His head snapped up, his eyes meeting mine with a mix of regret and frustration. "I know, alright? I know I fucked up. You think I don't see it every time I look at you?"

For a moment, the rawness in his voice cut through my defenses, but I couldn't let it show. I couldn't let him in, not again.

"Good," I said, standing abruptly and pushing my chair back. "Then maybe next time, you'll think twice before you decide to 'protect' someone by abandoning them."

I grabbed the map and turned toward the small desk in the corner, but Booker wasn't done.

"Mick," he said, his voice softer now. "I'm sorry. For everything."

I paused, my back to him, my fingers tightening on the edge of the map. For a moment, I considered turning around, letting him see the pain I still carried. But I couldn't.

"Sorry doesn't change anything," I said, my voice colder than I felt.

Booker didn't respond, and I didn't wait for him to.

Later that night, as I lay on the stiff bed, the weight of the conversation pressed down on me. Booker's words replayed in my mind, mingling with the memories I'd spent years trying to bury.

"I missed you."

"I thought I was protecting you."

With my hands clenched into tight fists, I stared up at the crumbling ceiling, frustration building inside me. Booker might have thought he was protecting me, but all he'd done was leave me to pick up the pieces of a life he'd shattered.

As I drifted into a restless sleep, one thought echoed in my mind: I wouldn't let Booker—or anyone else—break me again.

26

The Cuban heat clung to my skin as Booker and I navigated the narrow dirt road leading to Montgomery's compound. Ramón's map sat folded in my lap, every line and mark burned into my memory. The dense jungle around us felt alive, every rustle and whisper setting me on edge.

Booker sat behind the wheel, the steady roar of the engine the only sound between us. His hands gripped the steering wheel, his jaw tight as he scanned the road ahead. He'd been quiet the entire ride, his usual smirks and jabs replaced by determined focus that amplified the tension between us.

"You good?" he asked suddenly, his voice breaking the silence.

I glanced at him, catching the concern in his eyes. "I'm fine," I replied, though the knot in my stomach said otherwise.

Ahead, a checkpoint loomed, its makeshift barriers manned by two guards in fatigues. I adjusted my sunglasses, a plan already forming in my head. "Pull over just before we hit the bend," I said. "I'll handle this."

Booker's hand shot out to block me as I reached for the door.

"You sure about that? These aren't your average rent-a-cops."

I shot him a glare. "I don't need your approval, Booker. Stay ready in case things go sideways."

Stepping out, I felt the guards' eyes on me immediately. My heels crunched against the dirt as I approached, my hips swaying just enough to keep their attention where I wanted it. One of them stepped forward, his gaze dragging over me like I was a menu item.

"You lost, mami?" he asked, smirking.

I slipped off my sunglasses, meeting his eyes with a practiced smile. "Actually, I'm looking for someone. Maybe you can help me?"

I leaned in closer, letting the thin strap of my tank top slide slightly off my shoulder. His partner chuckled, leaning on his rifle as his eyes roved over me. Perfect.

Behind them, I saw Booker move. Silent, efficient, and fast. Before either man could react, he was on them, disarming one and delivering a swift blow to the other's temple. They crumpled to the ground, unconscious.

"Subtle."

He flashed a grin at me as he dusted off his hands. "You said to stay ready."

The guard's radios were smashed, their bodies hidden in the thick underbrush. As Booker and I slid into the car, the air seemed to thicken, creating a palpable sense of unease. He shifted into gear, the engine rumbling softly as we eased through the makeshift barrier. The dirt road ahead twisted into the jungle, the trees closing in around us like silent sentinels.

I glanced down at Ramón's map, the crude lines and markings suddenly feeling less like a guide and more like a gamble. The compound wasn't far now—maybe a mile—but every instinct I had screamed that something was wrong.

"You a'ight?" Booker asked.

"I'm fine," I said. "Just drive."

Booker shot me a sidelong glance but didn't press. The road narrowed, thick vegetation scraping against the car as we ventured further into the heart of the jungle. The air felt too still, too quiet, and I couldn't shake the feeling that we were being watched.

"There," Booker said, nodding toward a clearing ahead. A small wooden shack sat off to the side of the road, its tin roof rusted and sagging. A cluster of crates and barrels were stacked outside, and the faint smell of gasoline hung in the air.

"Checkpoint?" I asked, my hand instinctively reaching for the pistol holstered at my side.

"Could be," Booker said, his voice tight. "Or it could be something worse."

As we slowed to a crawl, the sound of voices reached us, muffled but growing louder. Booker killed the engine, and we sat in tense silence, listening. Through the dense foliage, I could make out the shapes of several men—six, maybe seven—moving between the shack and the road. They were armed, their rifles slung casually over their shoulders, but their movements were purposeful, motivated.

"Guards?" I whispered.

"More like reinforcements," Booker muttered. "This isn't on the map."

I glanced at him, my heart pounding. "What do we do?"

Booker leaned back in his seat, his eyes funneling as he assessed the situation. "We're outnumbered, and they've got the high ground. If they spot us, it's over."

"Then we don't let them spot us," I said, my mind racing. "We could—"

A sharp crack split the air, cutting me off. My head snapped toward the sound just in time to see one of the men point toward the car. He shouted something in Spanish, and within seconds, the entire group was moving toward us, their weapons raised.

"Shit," Booker hissed, slamming the car into reverse. The tires spun in the loose dirt before catching, and we lurched backward, the jungle rushing past in a blur.

Gunfire erupted behind us, the sharp cracks echoing through the trees. Bullets tore through the foliage, shattering branches and punching holes in the car's rear window. I ducked instinctively, my heart hammering in my chest.

"Drive!" I shouted, gripping the edge of my seat as Booker swung the car around, the tires skidding on the uneven road. He didn't need to be told twice. The engine roared as we sped back the way we came, the sound of gunfire fading into the distance.

By the time we reached the barrier, my hands were shaking,

my breath coming in short, shallow gasps. Booker didn't slow down, plowing through the makeshift blockade without hesitation. The guards we'd left unconscious were nowhere to be seen, and I didn't have time to wonder where they'd gone.

27

The sun was dipping below the horizon by the time we reached the safe house. My pulse was still racing as I stepped out of the car, the adrenaline that had kept me sharp during the escape now leaving me shaky and drained.

Booker slammed the car door behind him, his walk tense as he headed for the house. "We need a new plan," he said, his voice snappish.

"No shit," I retorted, following him inside.

The air in the safe house felt stifling, the silence pressing in around us as we moved into the small living room. I dropped the map onto the coffee table, my hands still trembling.

I stood by the window, my arms crossed as I watched the darkened streets outside. Booker paced behind me, his heavy footsteps the only sound in the room.

"They were waiting for us," My voice was sharp, the words tumbling out before I could temper them. "That wasn't just some random checkpoint. They knew someone was coming."

Booker sits on the couch, his elbows on his knees, his hands clasped tightly together. "Could've been a coincidence," he said, but the doubt in his tone betrayed him.

Turning to him, my eyes red with fury. "You don't believe that any more than I do. Someone tipped them off."

He looked up at me, his expression blank, but his silence spoke volumes. Finally, he asked the question that had been gnawing at both of us. "You think it was Bird?"

The name hung in the air like a storm cloud, heavy and ready to burst. I wanted to shake my head, to dismiss the idea outright, but I couldn't. Bird had set this whole thing in motion—the meeting with Ramón, the map, the contact for the house we were currently standing in. It all led back to her.

"I don't know," I admitted, the words tasting bitter on my tongue. "But if it was her…"

Booker leaned forward, his voice low but firm. "If it was her, then we're already in deeper than we thought."

The weight of his words slammed down on me. I sank into the chair opposite him, my mind racing. We were running out of time, out of options, and if Bird was playing both sides, it meant we were walking into something we might not survive.

Before either of us could say more, the door creaked open, and Bird stepped in, her presence filling the room like she owned it. She was dressed in a flowing yellow dress that clung to her curves, her gold jewelry catching the dim light. She looked every bit the part of someone who'd thrived in Havana's underworld—a queen in her own right.

"Well, don't everyone look so happy to see me," she said, her voice honeyed but arrogant as she closed the door behind her.

Booker's eyes narrowed as he stood, his body taut like a coiled spring. "What the hell are you doing here B?"

Bird raised an eyebrow, unbothered by his tone. "Handling business," she said smoothly. "Same as you."

"Business?" Booker shot back. "Funny how your 'business' seems to land us in the middle of an ambush."

Bird's expression didn't falter, but something shown in her eyes—annoyance, maybe even guilt. "What are you trying to say, Booker?"

"You tell me," he said, stepping closer. "You're the one with all the connections. How'd those guards know we were coming?"

I watched the exchange, my heart pounding. Part of me wanted to jump in, to defend Bird, but the other part—the part that couldn't ignore the sinking feeling in my gut—held me back.

Bird let out a soft laugh, shaking her head. "You really think I'd set you up? After everything?"

"You tell me," Booker repeated, his tone colder now.

Bird's gaze shifted to me, her eyes softening. "Mick, come on. You know me. You know I wouldn't do that to you."

Her words were like a dagger, twisting in my chest. I wanted to believe her—I needed to believe her. But the doubts were there, whispering in the back of my mind. "I want to believe you, Bird," I said quietly. "But this whole thing feels off."

She stepped closer, her tone more urgent now. "Look, I get it. It's messy, and yeah, maybe it's not going exactly as planned.

But I'm here for you, Mick. I'm trying to help you."

Booker let out a derisive snort, but I held up a hand, silencing him. "We need to loop Donovan in."

"You really think calling him is gonna fix this? He's in Miami, Mick. He's not the one walking into ambushes."

Before Booker could argue, I grabbed the phone from the coffee table and dialed the secure line Donovan had given us. It rang twice before his calm, steady voice came through.

"Talk to me," Donovan said, skipping the pleasantries.

"We've got a problem," I said, my tone clipped. "The route Ramón gave us wasn't clear. We hit a checkpoint, and it wasn't just a random patrol. They were waiting for us."

A pause. "How bad?"

"Bad enough that we had to abort," Booker cut in, his voice tense as he leaned against the back of the couch, hands stiff at his sides. "And now we're sitting here wondering if Bird's playing both sides."

There was a beat of silence on the other end—just long enough to let the weight of that statement land. When Donovan spoke again, his tone was sharper, colder. "Bird's not stupid. She knows what happens if she crosses you, Mick. What's her excuse?"

I turned to look at Bird, perched at the kitchen counter, sipping from a glass of wine like she wasn't the source of this chaos. "She says it was a misstep. Claims she has a contact who can get us closer to Montgomery. Someone named Enzo."

"Enzo?" Donovan repeated, and I could hear the skepticism

dripping through the line. "Why am I just now hearing about this?"

"That makes two of us," I said flatly, my eyes still fixed on Bird. "Apparently, he's been working for Montgomery for years. Runs a club in Old Havana that's a front for his operations."

Donovan's tone dropped to a hard edge, all pretense of calm gone. "And Bird thinks this guy's loyal?"

"She says he's not loyal, just greedy," I replied, though the words tasted sour in my mouth. "Claims he'll flip if we give him a better offer."

There was a longer silence. When Donovan spoke again, his voice was decisive, crisp. "You're not touching that club until I vet him."

Booker shot me a look, and I raised an eyebrow at the phone. "Vet him? From Miami?"

"You're forgetting who I am, Mikayla," Donovan replied coolly, the steel in his voice unmistakable. "I've got ears on the ground. I'll have my people dig into this Enzo. If he's dirty or playing both sides, I'll know before the sun comes up. You're too close to this. I'll handle it."

The relief was unspoken but real. Donovan never halfstepped anything, especially not for me. He didn't have to say it, but I knew—he'd always do whatever it took to protect me.

"You'll let us know as soon as you've got something?" I asked, my voice steadier than before.

"Of course," he said. "In the meantime, lay low. Don't move

on Enzo until I clear him. This operation is too damn close to going south."

Booker's voice cut in, rough and pointed. "What about you? You staying put in Miami?"

Donovan exhaled a sharp breath. "For now. I've got the safe house ready, but I'll keep an escape plan in place for you. If things get hot, I'll have a plane waiting. You'll come straight to me—no detours, no risks."

His tone softened just slightly as he addressed me directly. "Mick, trust your gut."

I swallowed hard, something twisting in my chest at his words.

"Thanks, Don," I said quietly.

"Just be careful," he replied. "Both of you."

I ended the call and set the phone down on the table, my hands still gripping it as though it might shatter if I let go. The weight of Donovan's words settling over me like a lead blanket. Trust your gut. My gut was telling me that something about Bird's story didn't add up, but I didn't have the luxury of walking away now. Not when we were this close.

Booker was watching me, his gaze steady but full of unspoken questions.

"He's vetting Enzo?" Booker asked.

I nodded, sinking into the armchair and letting out a slow breath. "Yeah. If this guy's dirty, Donovan will know."

"Good," Booker said, his voice rough. "Because I'm not walking into another trap. Not again."

KITTEN HEELS

"You want to tell me why we're just now hearing about this Enzo guy?" I asked Bird, who was still perched at the kitchen counter.

Bird looked up, her expression calm but guarded. "It wasn't relevant before."

"Not relevant?" Booker barked, pushing off the couch. "You don't think the guy who's supposedly gonna get us to Montgomery is relevant?"

Bird's gaze shot at him, unimpressed. "I didn't think we'd need him until now. Ramón's map was supposed to get you to the compound. If it had, we wouldn't even be having this conversation."

"But it didn't," I said, my voice cutting through the tension. "So start talking. Who is he?"

Bird set down her glass, her fingers tracing the rim as she spoke. "Enzo runs one of the hottest clubs in Old Havana. It's where Montgomery's people do a lot of their business—laundering money, cutting deals, you name it. Enzo's been working for him for years, but he's not loyal. He's in it for the money, the power. If we can offer him something better, he'll flip."

"And how do you know that?" Booker asked, crossing his arms.

Bird smirked, leaning back in her chair. "Because I know Enzo. We go way back."

"How far back?" I pressed, my suspicion growing.

"Far enough," Bird said, her tone dismissive. "He owes me a

favor, and he knows better than to cross me."

Booker scoffed, his disbelief evident. "So your plan is to waltz into this guy's club, cash in your favor, and hope he doesn't sell us out?"

Bird's smirk faded, her expression hardening. "My plan is to get you to Montgomery. That's why ya'll called me, right?"

"Enough," I said, stepping between them. "This conversation is over. Tomorrow we'll know more and go from there, until then, not another word from either of you." I snap.

The room felt heavier after Bird left, as if her presence lingered even though the door had closed behind her. Booker and I hadn't spoken much since then, both of us trying to pick apart the layers of this mess. The air between us was thick with more than just the tension of the mission. It was old wounds resurfacing, questions left unanswered, and truths that had yet to be spoken.

I sat back in the chair, my gaze fixed on the map spread out across the coffee table. Havana stared back at me—streets and alleys marked like veins of a city that felt more like a trap than a destination. Enzo's club, circled in red, sat there like a ticking bomb.

Booker stood near the window, his silhouette cutting against the moonlight. He looked as he always did—cool, composed—but I could see the tightness in his shoulders, the way his hand tapped restlessly against his thigh.

"You think Donovan's gonna find something on this Enzo?" Booker finally asked, his voice soft, almost cautious, like he didn't want to break whatever silence had settled between us.

"Maybe," I replied, though the word felt empty. "But even if he doesn't, I'm not trusting him. Something's off, Book. I can feel it."

Booker turned to face me, his dark eyes scanned mine, searching for something—an answer maybe, or a truth I wasn't ready to admit. "You still think it's Bird?"

I didn't answer immediately. My mind wandered back to her calm demeanor, her confident explanation of Enzo, and the way she carried herself like nothing could touch her. That was always Bird's greatest strength—making you believe she was untouchable while her hand was pulling every string in the background.

"I don't know yet," I admitted, though the unease churned inside me. "But we'll find out soon enough."

Booker pushed off the wall and moved to stand in front of me, his presence filling the space. "If it's her, we handle it. If it's Enzo, we handle it. Either way, we're getting Montgomery. You with me?"

I looked up at him, meeting his stare. There was something solid in the way he said it. For a moment, I let myself remember what it felt like to trust him. "I'm with you," I said quietly.

But as I dropped my eyes back to the map, the knot in my stomach tightened. Something wasn't right, and I wasn't sure what scared me more—the idea that Bird had turned on me or that there were things about this mission, about Booker, that I still didn't understand.

The silence stretched on for a beat longer than it should've, the air humming with the unsaid. Finally, I exhaled sharply, sitting up and leveling him with a stare. "Book… can I ask you something?"

He raised an eyebrow, slanting his head slightly. "Go ahead."

"Why are you here?" The words fell out of my mouth, heavier than I expected. "Why are you helping me with this? You haven't seen me in years, and yet here you are—following me into a city where you abandoned me nearly twenty years ago, risking your life. Helping me hunt down a man who… who betrayed me."

Booker looked away for a moment, his jaw stiffening as if he needed to brace himself. "You really wanna know?"

I folded my arms, unwilling to back down. "Yeah, Book. I do."

He turned back to me, his eyes suddenly softer, his usual cocky facade crumbling around the edges. "Because it's you, Mick."

The simple statement hit me like a kick to the belly.

"What's that supposed to mean?" I asked, trying to keep my voice leveled.

"It means…" Booker dragged a hand across the top of his head, his frustration slipping through. "It means I still owe you. For everything. For back then."

"Back then?" I shot back, my tone sharp now. "You mean back when you left me in Havana without so much as a goodbye? Back when you broke my damn heart and walked away like none of it meant anything?"

Booker flinched, just barely, but I caught it. He dropped his head, taking a deep breath before he looked at me again. This time, there was no bravado, no swagger. Just him.

"It wasn't like that," he said, his voice low but firm.

"Then what was it?" I demanded, leaning forward, pushing him for answers I'd buried years ago. "Tell me, Book, because I spent so much time trying to figure out why the hell you turned on me like that."

He stared at me for a long moment, and then, finally, he spoke. "I was protecting you."

There go those words again. "Protecting me?"

Booker let out a humorless laugh, the sound rough, like gravel underfoot. He shook his head, his hands flexing restlessly at his sides. "Yeah. You think I wanted to leave you, Mick? You think it didn't tear me apart to walk away? I had no choice."

His voice caught, and for a moment, I saw something in his face I hadn't seen in years—pain. The kind that runs deep and never really leaves you. The kind that lingers like smoke after a fire.

"What choice?" I demanded, my voice harsh, though my hands trembled in my lap. "You don't just walk away from someone without a word, Book. That's not a choice—it's a betrayal."

Booker's gaze snapped up to meet mine, his jaw tight as if he were holding something back, but then, like a dam breaking, it came rushing out.

"The night after that deal with Valdés, I got a call. Big Sal. He said one of our trap houses in Harlem got lit up. Bullets everywhere. It wasn't random, Mick. It wasn't a message to me—it was a message to you."

My breath caught, freezing me in place. "Me?"

He nodded, his face darkening. "Yeah. The crew that hit it? They thought it was your call. Blood for blood."

The air seemed to vanish from the room. My pulse roared in my ears, my mind racing to piece together memories I'd buried. "When we got back, I knew one of our houses got hit, but you never told me you knew why."

"How could I?" Booker's voice rose, raw and unsteady, his frustration bubbling over. "How was I supposed to tell you that it was because of me? That I was the reason they were coming for you?"

"What the hell are you talking about, Booker?" I felt off balanced, like the floor beneath me was shifting.

Booker let out a breath, his shoulders slumping as if the weight of what he was about to say had finally beaten him down. He turned away from me, his voice quieter but no less powerful.

"Before Havana," he started, staring at the far wall like he could see the past playing out in front of him, "I went to see Stone in Rikers. He'd been hearing whispers from inside—someone still owed him. A guy who hadn't paid his dues and thought he could slide by under the radar. Stone wanted me to handle it. And I did."

He turned back to me, his glare haunted, and for a second, I almost didn't recognize him. The cocky, untouchable prince of the streets was gone. The man before me seemed crushed under the weight of his own guilt, burdened by the decisions he had made that forever altered both of our lives.

"What did you do?" I asked, my voice barely above a whisper.

Booker exhaled hard, running his hands over his face as if trying to scrub the memory away. "I put him down, Mick. Just like Stone wanted. The problem was that crew thought you called the hit. They thought it was retaliation for something they'd done, and they weren't about to let it slide."

I stared at him, my chest tight, trying to process what he was telling me. "So the house…"

He nodded grimly. "Yeah. When the trap house got hit, they were sending a message to you. If we'd been back in Harlem, you would've been there. You always were. And I couldn't…" His voice cracked, just slightly, but he pushed through. "I couldn't let them come for you. I couldn't let you get caught in the crossfire because of something I did."

Silence blanketed the room, thick and suffocating. My mind replayed everything—Havana, Booker's sudden coldness, the way he'd left me. The way he'd broken me. I'd spent so long thinking it had been about me. That I hadn't been enough. That he hadn't loved me the way I loved him. But now…

"You thought leaving me would protect me?" My voice trembled, and I hated how small it sounded.

Booker dropped his head, his voice hoarse. "Yeah. I thought

if I pushed you away—if I made you hate me—it would keep you safe. I was trying to save you, Mick. But I wasn't just breaking your heart. I was breaking mine, too."

I swallowed hard, my chest tightening so much it felt like I couldn't breathe. For years, I'd carried the weight of that night, the sting of his betrayal. I'd built walls around myself, turned the pain into armor, made myself into someone untouchable. A bad bitch who didn't need anyone. But standing here, hearing this, the years I spent fortifying myself felt meaningless now. The walls I'd relied on suddenly trembling like brittle glass.

"Why didn't you tell me?" I asked softly.

Booker took a step closer, his dark eyes locking onto mine. "Because you were better off without me. You had a future, Mick. College, freedom—everything I couldn't give you. You didn't need me dragging you back into the dirt."

I stared at him, seeing him in a way I hadn't before. Not just as the boy who'd loved me and left me, but as a man carrying the weight of decisions no twenty-year-old should've had to make. Decisions he'd made for me.

All this time, I'd thought I was the one who'd been left behind. I hadn't realized how much it had cost him to let me go.

"You thought you were protecting me," I said softly, the realization sinking in like a knife.

"I didn't see another way." He nodded

I looked down, my hands shaking as I rolled them into fists. All these years, I'd been running. Running from Havana, running from Booker, running from the truth about who I really was. I thought I'd been building myself into something stronger, someone better, but now I wasn't so sure. Maybe I had just been wearing high heels and playing the part of a bad bitch. Maybe all this time, I've just been a hurt little girl who never really healed- walking through life, pretending.

When I looked back at Booker, the man I'd loved for so long, I saw the truth in his eyes. He'd been trying to save me. And in his own way, maybe he had.

The distance between us seemed to shrink, the years of pain and anger peeling away gently, falling away like the petals of a wilting flower. Booker stepped forward, his hand hovering near mine, as if unsure whether I'd let him close.

"Mick…" he started, his voice deep and low.

I didn't let him finish. I stepped toward him, closing the distance, and grabbed the front of his shirt, pulling him down into me. Our lips crashed together, the kiss rough, raw—years of tension and longing boiling over.

His hands found my waist, pulling me closer, and I didn't fight it. For once, I let myself feel it—the love, the pain, the weight of everything we'd been through.

He pulled back just enough to look into my eyes, his forehead resting against mine. "I'm sorry," he whispered, the words heavy with meaning.

"I know," I whispered back. "I know."

For the first time in years, the pieces of me that had been broken didn't feel so jagged anymore. For the first time, I wasn't running. I was here. With him.

28

The sun rose slowly, creeping through the cracks in the old curtains, casting faint streaks of gold across the room. I lay there, tangled in the sheets, Booker's steady breathing next to me. The night before felt like a dream—like stepping into a time when things were simple, when I wasn't carrying the weight of the streets, the betrayals, or the hunt for a man who had turned my world upside down.

Booker stirred, his arm brushing against me. I froze. For a brief second, I thought about staying—just staying in this moment forever. Safe. Untouched. Wrapped in the peace that came when I wasn't fighting to prove myself, fighting for survival, or chasing ghosts.

But I wasn't that girl anymore. I hadn't been her in a long time.

I slipped out of bed quietly, gathering my clothes from where they'd been discarded. My muscles ached in a way that wasn't just physical, and as I stood in front of the small bathroom mirror, I stared at the woman looking back at me. For the first time in years, I felt a glimpse of calm, a crack in the armor I'd spent so long building.

But peace? I didn't trust it. Not yet. Not here.

Pulling my hair back into a tight ponytail, I pushed the doubts down. I wasn't here for peace. I wasn't here for Booker. I was here for him.

Raul. Jason. Montgomery—whatever you want to call him.

I turned on the tap, splashing cold water on my face. My reflection didn't soften; it hardened. I wasn't about to lose myself again. I had one job, and the closer I got to finding him, the more I questioned whether it was even worth it. What was I chasing? Revenge? Answers? Maybe I didn't want to know why Raul picked me, why he lied, and why he turned my life into this chaotic mess. Maybe all I wanted was to erase him.

I stepped back into the room to find Booker sitting on the edge of the bed, already dressed, lacing up his boots. His gaze lifted to meet mine, and for a moment, the easy intimacy from last night lingered in the air like a sweet fragrance.

"Morning," he said, his voice husky.

"Morning," I echoed, struggling to keep my tone detached.

He studied me, a small smile yanking at his lips. "You look like you're about to run out of here."

I smirked, slipping on my sneakers. "Maybe I am."

"Cold-blooded," Booker teased, though his eyes softened. "You good?"

"Yeah." I grabbed my jacket and slid my arms into it. "I'm fine."

But I wasn't. Not really.

The burner phone buzzed on the table just as we made our way into the small kitchen area of the safe house. Booker snatched it up first, eyeing the number before handing it over.

"It's Donovan."

I exhaled, steadying myself as I answered. "What you got?"

Donovan's voice came through the line, calm and measured, yet laced with an underlying urgency. "I've got intel on your boy Enzo and some... unexpected news about Bird."

I stiffened. "Go on."

"First, Enzo checks out—he runs the Surco y Toque club in Old Havana. The club's where Jason handles the bulk of his business. If you want to get close to him, that's your way in."

"Got it," I said, my voice clipped. "What about Bird?"

There was a pause. Then Donovan's voice dropped, as if he was about to tell me something he didn't want to say. "Mick, Booker's suspicions were right. Bird's been living large in Havana for years now, and not just on her husband's baseball money. She's got her hands in everything. She has connections with the underworld—deep connections. And here's the kicker: she's the reason Raul found you."

"What?" The words hitting me like a bullet to the chest.

"You heard me," Donovan said firmly. "Bird met Raul in New York, not long after you left for Atlanta. She was still mad, still holding a grudge because you left her behind. Your name carried weight in the streets, and without you, she wasn't getting the respect she thought she deserved. Raul saw her anger. He saw her need to prove herself. So, she helped him. She facilitated him."

My mind spun, struggling to process his words. "Facilitated him how?"

"She cultivated him, Mick. That's what she does—she builds people up, gives them the tools to succeed. Raul was already a hustler and a con, but Bird made him sharper. Better. And when he was ready, she pointed him at you."

I collapse into a chair, my hands reaching for something to hold on to as nausea rolled through me. "Why me?"

"Because you were the queen, Mikayla. The princess of the streets. Taking you down wasn't just about money for Raul—it was about power. And for Bird, it was about revenge."

Booker's eyes were on me now, piercing and worried. "What's going on?" he asked.

I shook my head, unable to look at him just yet. "What else?" I asked Donovan, my voice strained.

"That's all I've got for now, but listen to me, Mick. Bird's been working this angle for a long time. Don't underestimate her, and don't assume she's on your side. You're walking into a snake pit, and she's holding the gate open for you."

The line went dead, and the room fell silent.

I sat at the edge of the worn kitchen chair, my elbows on my knees, staring at the floor as though it could give me answers. My pulse was steady, but the rage underneath clawed at my ribs, begging to break free. I let out a slow breath, trying to collect myself, but my hands find themselves curling into fists anyway.

Booker moved closer, crouching in front of me. "What did he say?"

I didn't answer right away. Instead, I get up and paced a few steps, the floorboards creaking beneath me. My mind spun with rage, betrayal, and something deeper I couldn't name. When I finally stopped, I looked him dead in the eye.

"It was Bird," I said, my voice low but cold. "She's the reason Raul found me. She set me up."

Booker's jaw twitched, his brow furrowing, and for a second, he looked as if he didn't want to believe it. But suspicion had already been there, lurking. "You sure?"

I nodded slowly, swallowing down the knot in my throat. "Donovan laid it all out. Bird met Raul back in New York, not long after I left. She resented me for leaving her behind—for taking the crown and leaving her to clean up the pieces. She found Raul and turned him into what he is now. That's what she does, Book and I... I was just the mark."

"Mick—"

"I need to see her," I cut in, my voice hard and decisive.

He stepped forward, closer to me. "And what does 'see her' mean?"

"It means I need to handle it," I said coolly, meeting his gaze without flinching.

"Handle it?" His voice coated with warning. "You mean you're gonna confront her. Alone."

"Yeah. Alone." I turned away from him. My hands felt steadier now that I'd made up my mind. I needed to look Bird in the face. I needed to see her, to hear her excuses—if she even bothered with them. I needed to know why. And then I'd handle it.

Booker stepped in front of me before I could move past him, his voice dropping. "Mick, think about this. Bird's dangerous now. She's playing in Raul's world, and you don't know what she's capable of."

"I know exactly what she's capable of," I shot back, my eyes narrowing. "She pointed a snake in my direction and walked away without looking back. I can't let this slide Book."

His expression grew rigid, frustration visible in his eyes. "And what happens when you roll up on her, huh? What if she's got people watching? You're walking into her territory blind."

"Then I'll handle it." My voice was steady, but my tone was sharp as glass. I moved past him, but he caught my wrist, his grip gentle but firm.

"Mick, don't shut me out," he said, his voice quieter now. "You said I'm with you, right? So let me be with you."

I turned to face him, softening just enough for him to see it. "You are with me, Book. But I need to do this. Alone."

His mouth flexed, his hand releasing me reluctantly. "Fine," he said finally, stepping back. "But we're not staying here. If Bird's people got us this place, it means we're burned. I'll find us somewhere else to lay low."

"Do that." I said, brushing past him toward the door.

He followed me, his footsteps heavy. "If you're not back in two hours, Mick, I'm coming for you."

I glanced back at him, allowing a sliver of a smirk to lift one corner of my mouth. "You won't need to."

The morning air was crisp as I stepped outside, the sunlight cutting through the lingering chill. The street beyond the safe house was quiet, still waking up, but it felt too open, too exposed. I didn't look back as I made my way to the car, the engine growling to life beneath my hands.

I drove through the half-empty streets, Havana sprawled out before me like a painting of secrets. The sun was climbing, too bright, too beautiful for what I was about to do. But I didn't care.

Bird was waiting for me.

And I was ready.

29

The drive to Bird's mansion was slow and winding, each mile giving me too much time to think. The roads were empty, the early morning light bathing everything in a washed-out gray. My knuckles were white against the wheel as I gripped it tighter, trying to keep my mind steady.

Bird.

The name sat heavy on my tongue, like bile I couldn't swallow. She had been everything once—my confidant, my mentor, my family. I could still hear her voice hyping me up as a teenager: "You're the queen, Mick. Don't let anyone tell you otherwise." And I hadn't. I wore the crown she placed on my head, the same crown she resented me for.

I pulled up to the house, its cold grandeur standing tall against the edge of the cliff. It felt more like a mausoleum than a mansion now, a shrine to a woman who'd clawed her way to the top only to lose her soul along the way. The driveway was empty. No cars. No voices. Just the restless sound of waves crashing against the rocks below.

The front door was unlocked—always a sign. I didn't

hesitate. I stepped inside, my heels clicking against the polished marble like gunshots in the stillness.

"Bird!" My voice echoed, sharp and deliberate.

Silence.

I moved deeper, past the sterile living room with its floor-to-ceiling windows and the designer furniture no one ever sat on. This was a house meant to be seen, not lived in.

The glass doors to the patio were cracked open, the breeze carrying in the salty tang of the sea. I stepped outside, and there she was—lying on a chaise lounge near the railing, her white dress rippling in the wind. She had a tumbler of bourbon dangling from her fingertips, and for a moment, she looked peaceful. Like she belonged here.

She didn't turn as I approached. "Took you long enough," she said, her voice as smooth as it always was, but with an edge sharp enough to cut with.

I stopped a few feet from her, my arms crossed tight over my chest. "You knew I was coming."

"Course I did," she replied, finally setting the glass down and turning to face me. "You always did like to settle your scores face-to-face."

"How long?" My voice trembled with restrained fury. "How long have you been playing me, Bird?"

She smirked faintly, but there was no humor in it. "Playing you? Don't flatter yourself, Mick. You think this is all about you? Nah. This is about me."

"Bullshit," I snapped, stepping closer. "You handed me to

KITTEN HEELS

Raul. You pointed him at me. Family doesn't do that, Bird!"

Her smirk faltered, her jaw tightening. "Family? Don't throw that word at me like it means something. Where was family when you left me, huh? When you ran off to Spelman and left me to pick up your scraps?"

"I earned that escape, Bird. You could've come with me."

"Come with you?" Her voice rose, iced and bitter. "To what? Be your shadow? Be the sidekick while you got your fresh start? No, Mick. I stayed behind because this life was all I had. And when you left, the streets didn't remember me—they just remembered you. I wasn't good enough without you."

I felt like she'd slapped me, her words a punch to my gut. "So what? You decided to sell me out to Raul? You wanted revenge? You wanted to ruin me?"

She scoffed, stepping closer until we were nearly chest to chest. "I didn't sell you out. I gave him a name. I gave him an opportunity. You think you're the only one who can hustle, Mick? You're not the queen anymore. You're just a relic of the past, trying to claw your way back to a throne no one remembers."

The words cut deep, but they fueled the fire burning inside me. My fingers twitched at my sides. "You betrayed me," I said, my voice cold and measured. "After everything we went through. After everything I gave you."

Bird stared at me, her face a mask of both fury and hurt. "I gave you, too, Mick. I gave you you. You wouldn't be who you are if I hadn't been there, building you up while you played dress-up in your daddy's empire. You're Stone's daughter, yeah, but I'm the one who made you."

I felt the truth of her words, but they didn't absolve her. "And look where that got us," I said quietly.

We stared at each other for a long, tense moment. Years of history, loyalty, and bitterness boiled down to this single breath of silence.

"What now?" Bird finally asked, her voice quieter but no less sharp. "You gonna put me down like one of your daddy's enemies?"

"I don't have a choice," I said, and I meant it. I had crossed too many lines already. Letting her walk away—family or not—would make me weak, and I couldn't afford that.

Her lips curled into a sad, knowing smile. "I figured as much."

Before I could even react, she was on me. Bird moved with an animalistic speed, faster than I ever could've imagined. Her hands were like claws, grabbing, pulling, raking at me. I stumbled backward, the force of her shove knocking me off-balance. My heel skidded on the slick patio, the smooth surface betraying me. I felt my chest tighten, the ground slipping away beneath me—but instinct took over. I twisted, just in time to lock my fingers around her wrist, using the momentum to spin her toward the railing.

"Don't make me do this, Bird!" I shouted, my voice strained, my breath ragged in my throat.

She smirked, her lips curling into a bitter, mocking grin.

"You ain't built for this, Mick! You never were!" She fought against my grip, her body thrashing, desperate to break free. Her words cut deeper than I wanted to admit.

The rage inside me flared, hot and vicious. With a force I didn't even know I had shoved her into the railing. The moment her body collided with the glass, a sharp, sickening crack shattered the stillness of the night. The sound was deafening, the glass groaning under her weight, cracking like a thousand tiny stars exploding in the darkness. Her eyes widened, the shock and realization sinking in as the once-sturdy barrier trembled, then shattered completely, collapsing beneath the pressure.

For a heartbeat, time seemed to stretch, as if the world itself had paused. We locked eyes—hers still blazing with stubborn defiance, mine burning with fury, betrayal.

"Mick—"

The glass shattered, and Bird fell. The scream tore from her throat before the wind swallowed it whole. I stood frozen, panting, as I heard the sickening crash of her body against the rocks below.

The wind howled around me, the ocean roaring louder than it had moments before. I forced my breathing to slow, forced my hands to steady. There was no time for tears. No time for grief.

I moved quickly, retracing my steps through the house. I wiped down every surface I had touched, careful not to leave a trace. In the corner of the foyer, I spotted the security system.

My fingers flew over the controls, my pulse hammering in my ears as I wiped out every clip of me coming into or moving through the house.

When the files were gone, I pulled a scarf over my hands to press the power button, shutting the system down completely.

No evidence. No trail.

I took one last look at the mansion as I stepped out the front door. The house was still silent, still pristine. Bird had been right about one thing: she made me. But now, I had ended her.

I slid into the car, the hum of the engine breaking the quiet. My hands grip the steering wheel, steady now. My chest was tight, my throat burning, but I couldn't cry. Not now.

But as I pulled away, leaving Bird and the life she'd built behind me, I couldn't shake the feeling that something inside me had shattered too.

Bird was gone. The streets would whisper her name, but they wouldn't know what happened. They wouldn't know it was me.

But I would.

30

How could I?

The thought twisted like a knife in my heart.

How couldn't I?

Bird had betrayed me. She'd been the one to point Raul at me, the one who sold me out for reasons that burned more than the betrayal itself. Resentment. That was her currency. I'd left her to fend for herself, not realizing the streets would chew her up and spit her out once I was gone. I should've known better.

Everyone in my family betrayed me in some way.

Harriet. Stone. And now Bird.

The reflection of the road blurred in my vision as a single tear slipped free. I blinked it back angrily, forcing my focus on the drive. I couldn't afford to break. Not now.

Booker's coded message flashed on the burner phone sitting in the passenger seat. Coordinates. Directions to a new safe house. I had told him to handle it, and as always, he had. A man of his word, for better or worse.

But as the miles passed, my mind betrayed me, dragging me back to a different time. A time when trust wasn't something

I questioned, when loyalty wasn't a weapon to stab you in the back.

The house buzzed with a kind of energy you could feel in your bones—laughter, music, the soft pop of champagne corks, and the low purr of an R&B classic drifting through the speakers. Nights like this were like not even the universe couldn't reach us.

I leaned against the granite kitchen counter, barefoot and clutching a glass of champagne, my eyes following Booker as he poured another round. He looked proud—like a king surveying his castle, his grin cocky and contagious.

"Seattle locked in. Paper straight. What else do we need?" he said, holding his glass high.

Donovan, posted comfortably in the corner with his sleeves rolled up and his tie hanging loose, raised his glass. The new Captain Donovan. He had just made rank, a move none of us were surprised by. That man had been walking a fine line his whole life—keeping one foot in the streets with us while the other climbed ladder after ladder in the NYPD.

"To expansion. To growth. And to the fact that we're not all in jail," Donovan said, his voice playful but honest.

"Yet," Bird quipped as she strutted into the room, a bottle of bourbon tucked under her arm. Her smile was bright and inviting, hair in soft waves, gold hoop earrings big enough to signal from space. Bird had a way of owning a room without saying much at all—her swagger, her style, her whole aura.

"Bourbon?" Booker teased, smirking as he held up the

champagne bottle. "We got classy shit tonight, Bird."

"Champagne's for y'all," Bird shot back, setting the bourbon down with a satisfying thud. "I drink real shit."

Her gaze locked on me, and for just a moment, the smirk softened. There was something in her eyes—pride, satisfaction. I knew that look well. Bird saw me as her reflection, her proof that her game was stronger than anyone else's.

"Don't let her fool you," I said, laughing, the champagne bubbles tickling my nose. "She's just mad she didn't get here first."

Bird rolled her eyes, but the grin stayed. "Girl, don't act brand new. I'm the reason you're here. I put you on. I made you."

It was a joke on the surface, but there was no denying the truth underneath. Bird had made me. She was the one who taught me how to move like a queen, to walk into rooms full of men and leave them speechless. She made sure I was untouchable, undeniable. We had been two sides of the same coin. Until I outgrew her, and everything changed.

"Y'all acting like we're not at the top," Booker said as he strolled over and slid an arm around my waist. His presence was easy then—comfortable and familiar, like we were carved out of the same mold. We were a team, unstoppable together, and that night it felt like we couldn't lose.

"Years ago, none of us would've thought we'd be here," Donovan said, his voice cutting through the noise. He wasn't smiling anymore. "We're a team. But don't forget that this shit can fall apart just as fast as we built it."

"Damn D, always gotta ruin the vibe," Booker grumbled, pulling me closer as if to protect me from Donovan's warning.

Bird snorted, tossing back a shot of bourbon like it was water. "He's not wrong, though. The streets don't love you forever. You gotta take your wins while you can."

I looked around the room at all of them—Booker, Donovan, Bird. My family. The people who had carried me, built me, and who I thought I would stand beside forever. We were all so young, so certain we could outsmart the game.

Bird grinned at me, a gleam of mischief in her eye. "Mick, tell me this don't feel right. Like we're unstoppable."

"Unstoppable?" I echoed, clinking my glass with hers. "We are unstoppable."

I meant it. At the time, I believed it. We all did.

But sitting there, watching Donovan loosen his tie while sipping champagne like he wasn't one of the most powerful men in the NYPD, and Booker celebrating our latest expansion, and Bird grinning like she owned the world—I didn't see the cracks forming underneath us. The pride, the ambition, the secrets none of us were ready to admit.

We thought we had time.

We thought we had each other.

In that moment, we were invincible.

I blinked as the memory dissolved, my heart aching in a way I hadn't felt in years. That memory cut deep. Family. That's what we used to be. Before Donovan was "Mayor Donovan," before Bird turned on me, before Booker walked away. Back then, we celebrated like kings and queens because we thought we'd earned it.

Now look at us.

I reached up to wipe the tear trailing down my cheek, cursing myself for even letting it fall. That version of me—the one who could be soft, who could celebrate, who could believe in loyalty—she was dead and buried.

I exhaled sharply, gripping the wheel harder. Focus.

Donovan.

My grip on the wheel tightened, the car swerving slightly as suspicion gnawed at me again. Donovan told me to call Bird. He didn't have the intel? Didn't know she was playing me? That wasn't like him. Donovan always knew.

With a quick glance at the road, I grabbed the burner phone and dialed.

"Talk to me," Donovan answered after the second ring.

"You knew Bird was here," I said, my voice cold, accusatory. "You're the one who told me to call her. How the hell didn't you know she was working with Raul?"

A beat of silence. Donovan's voice dropped, steady but firm. "Watch where you're going with this, Mikayla."

"You're dodging," I shot back, anger bubbling up. "You always know everything. You're two steps ahead before the rest of us even make a move. So how did this slip through?"

His tone sharpened. "You think I'm in on it? You think I sent you into that? Do you think I'd do that to you?"

I forced myself to swallow, my anger faltering, but the paranoia didn't loosen its grip. "Then explain it to me. Why didn't you know?"

"Because Bird went deeper than I thought," Donovan said, his voice hard. "She had covered her tracks so well, I thought she was just a housewife with connections here and there, I didn't realize how deep she ran until I was looking into Enzo's known associates, and everything unraveled."

His words struck something inside me, the certainty in his tone a tether I didn't know I needed.

"I don't know who to trust anymore, Don," I admitted, my voice shaking.

Silence crackled between us, the weight of my accusation hanging heavy. When Donovan spoke again, his voice was controlled, but there was pain there, too.

"I've kept you alive since you were a kid, Mick," he said quietly. "I've been your shield in ways you'll never know. Don't insult me by thinking I'd set you up."

His words sliced through the whirlpool of frustration and doubt that had been swirling in my mind. I exhaled, my shoulders relaxing just slightly.

"I don't know, Donovan," I admitted, softer now. "I just… I can't see straight. I don't know who's with me and who's not."

"You trust yourself," he said firmly. "You trust me. And you keep moving. You don't stop until this is done. You didn't get this far by folding under pressure."

"I'll call you when I link with Booker." The knot in my throat loosening.

"Be careful," he said before the line went dead.

I tossed the phone back onto the seat and stared straight ahead, the horizon blurring through the windshield. Donovan's words reverberated inside me, but they didn't erase the unease sitting heavy in my gut.

I had one foot back in the game the moment I landed in New York. But now, after what I'd done to Bird, I was fully back in it—blood on my hands and nowhere to turn.

This wasn't about Raul anymore. This was about me—about who I was, who I'd tried to become, and the person I was realizing I could never truly bury.

31

The drive to the new safe house felt like a blur, the road stretching endlessly before me. My chest felt heavy, like every mile I put between Bird's mansion and myself only weighed me down more. The ocean breeze couldn't wash away what I'd done. My mind was a mess of static—a loop of Bird's face, her final scream, the sound of the glass shattering.

And Donovan. His voice echoed in my head, sharp and accusatory, even though I had been the one pointing fingers. Accusing him. Doubting him.

I'd broken something today. I didn't know how to piece myself back together, didn't even know where to start.

The sun had long since dipped below the horizon by the time I reached the house. It was tucked into the hills, cloaked in darkness, surrounded by thick underbrush.

I killed the engine and sat there for a moment, staring at the faint glow of light coming from inside. I thought about turning around. I thought about driving until the gas ran out. But I didn't. I couldn't. Booker was waiting.

The wooden floorboards creaked beneath my boots as I stepped inside. Booker was there, standing in the middle of the room like he'd been pacing for hours. His dark eyes snapped to mine, scanning me quickly before narrowing.

"You're late," he said, his voice low but edged with worry.

I dropped my bag onto the floor and shrugged off my jacket. "Traffic."

"Mick."

The way he said my name made me freeze. Soft. Like he knew. Like he could see straight through me.

"You good?" he asked like he always did when he seen through my façade.

I didn't answer. I couldn't. I tossed my jacket onto a chair and moved to the far side of the room, keeping the distance between us. Booker didn't move, but I felt his stare burning into my back.

"How did it go?" he asked quietly. "With Bird."

The question hit like a punch to the chest. My shoulders stiffened, but I didn't turn around.

"It's done," I said flatly.

"That's not what I asked."

I turned slowly, meeting his gaze. Booker's face was unreadable, but there was something in his eyes—concern, maybe even suspicion. The air between us was heavy, tense. For a moment, I thought about telling him the truth. I thought about telling him how Bird fell, how her scream followed me all the way here. But the words caught in my throat.

"Let it go, Booker," I said, my voice sharper than I intended. "It's done."

He stared at me for a long moment, his jaw tightening. "You don't have to carry this alone, Mick."

I let out a humorless laugh, forcing my gaze back to his. "Is that right? Last I checked, I've been carrying everything alone for years. Why stop now?"

Booker's expression faltered, and for a split second, I thought I saw something flicker there—hurt, maybe. But it was gone just as quickly, replaced by that same quiet intensity. The lingering tension between us crackled in the air like static—unspoken, unresolved. The night we'd spent together felt like a line we'd crossed, but neither of us knew what lay on the other side.

"Book, we've got more important things to deal with right now." I stated softly, releasing my hair from its tie and letting it fall against my shoulders.

He stepped back, conceding. "Fine. But you're not brushing me off forever, Mick. You can pretend you're made of stone all you want, but I know you."

Maybe he did. Maybe that's what scared me the most.

We didn't waste time. Booker and I moved quickly, grabbing the blueprints of Enzo's club Donovan had sent over and our gear before heading out into Havana's morning bustle. The streets were alive with the sounds of car horns, vendors shouting their wares, and music spilling from open doorways. It was a sharp contrast to the silence I carried inside me.

I sat in the passenger seat as Booker navigated through the winding streets, my focus locked on the plan forming in my mind.

"Surco y Toque," I said, breaking the silence. "Front for Montgomery's operations, and Bird…" I trailed off, my throat tightening. "Bird claimed Enzo's been Raul's right hand for years."

Booker glanced at me. "You trust any of that? After what happened?"

"I don't trust anything anymore," I muttered, shifting in my seat. "But it doesn't matter. Enzo's our only lead, and he's close to Raul. That's all we need to know."

"And what's the play when we get inside?" Booker's voice was calm, but I could hear the anxiety beneath it. "We're not walking in guns blazing, so what's your angle?"

I turned to him, arching a brow. "I get close to Enzo."

His hands tightened on the steering wheel. "Close? What do you mean close?"

I ignored the edge in his voice, focusing instead on the details of the plan. "He runs that club, which means he likes attention. Men like Enzo always think they're the smartest guy in the room. I'll make him feel like he's right."

"You're going to play him," Booker said flatly, though it wasn't a question.

I shrugged, smoothing my hands down the front of my jacket. "It's what I do best. I'll flirt, get him comfortable, and find a way to get his phone. If I can copy everything off it,

Donovan can run the data and find Montgomery."

Booker's jaw flexed, his dark eyes cutting over to me. "That's risky as hell, Mick. You don't know what kind of guy Enzo really is."

"Doesn't matter," I shot back. "I'll handle it."

"You're walking into the lion's den." His voice rose slightly, frustration simmering under his calm exterior. "What if he figures out you're playing him? What if—"

I turned in my seat, cutting him off. "Then I'll improvise. I've been doing this a long time, Book. I'm not some damsel who needs saving."

He exhaled through his nose, shaking his head as he pulled into a side street a few blocks from the club. "I'm just saying, I don't like it."

"Noted," I said coolly, reaching into my bag to retrieve my phone and a sleek, black device Donovan had sent with the blueprints. It was small—barely the size of a lighter—but powerful. "This'll let me mirror everything on his phone. Calls, messages, files. If he's in touch with Raul, this will give us a direct link."

Booker parked the car and turned to me, his gaze hard. "And you think Enzo's just going to hand over his phone?"

"No," I said, slipping the device into my pocket. "That's why I'll take it."

We stood across the street from Surco y Toque, a low-slung building with blacked-out windows and a heavy iron door flanked by two men who looked more like bouncers for a fight club than a nightclub. The heat pressed down on my shoulders, but I barely felt it. My mind was already ahead, mapping out every step.

"You sure about this?" Booker asked, his voice low as he adjusted his jacket to conceal his weapon.

I pulled a compact mirror from my bag, swiping a deep red lipstick across my lips and blotting once. "I'm sure."

Booker's gaze lingered on me, searching. "You good, Mick? You're not usually this… amped up before a job."

I turned to face him, meeting his stare head-on. "Don't worry about me, Book. Just keep your eyes open and your gun ready. Stay close, but don't make yourself obvious. I'll signal if I need you."

He didn't argue, but I could see it in his face—he knew something had shifted in me. I wasn't just back in the game. I was all in. Bird's blood might as well have been the ink that sealed the deal. There was no turning back now.

"Copy that," he said, though his jaw remained tight.

I straightened my shoulders and walked toward the entrance, my heels clicking against the cracked pavement. The guards watched me approach, their gazes heavy, but I welcomed it, pulling out a sultry smile like a weapon.

"Buenos días," I purred, sliding my sunglasses down just enough to make eye contact. "I'm here to see Enzo."

The larger of the two guards grunted. "Enzo doesn't take visitors."

I tilted my head, letting my smile widen. "He'll want to see me."

"Why's that?"

I stepped closer, dropping my voice just enough to sound conspiratorial. "Because I'm worth his time."

The two men exchanged a look before the smaller one cracked the door open. "Stay here."

I stood there, my hands gliding down my fitted dress that accentuated my curves and kept the other guard's attention on me. A minute later, the door opened wider, and I was waved inside.

The club was dark and sweltering, the air heavy with the scent of sweat, cologne, and stale cigars. Soft Latin music played from unseen speakers, giving the place an eerie calm, but I could feel it—the danger lurking beneath the surface.

The role fits me like a second skin, seamless and effortless. My heels struck the floor with perfect precision, each step a masterstroke of calculation. Enzo watched, his gaze dripping with the arrogance of a man who believed he was beyond reach.

Booker, unseen in the shadows near the bar, was watching too. I could feel it—the heat of his gaze on me, the tension radiating from him like a live wire ready to spark.

I couldn't let myself think about him. Not now.

Enzo's smile widened as I leaned just close enough to pull him in, my voice low and silken. "I've heard about you, Enzo. Word travels fast when you're as powerful as you are."

His eyes gleamed, eating up the flattery like I knew he would. Men like Enzo didn't need facts. They needed worship. "And what exactly did you hear?"

"That you're the man who makes things happen. The man with connections." I let my lips curve into a slow, knowing smile as I trailed a fingertip along the edge of the table. "And I need a man like that."

Enzo laughed softly, leaning back into the leather loveseat like a king on his throne. "You've got my attention, hermosa. What kind of connections are you looking for?"

"The kind that involve power, money, and discretion. I'm looking to set up something... long-term. I like being in control, and I don't trust many people to help me with that."

He raised a brow, intrigued. "You sound like a woman who knows exactly what she wants."

"I do." I glanced down briefly, as if shy—just for a second—before locking eyes with him again. "But a woman like me needs the right... partner."

His smile turned predatory, and I knew I had him. Enzo was walking right into my trap, blind to it all. His pride, his arrogance—it was a reflection I knew how to manipulate.

As I leaned back in my seat, Enzo's smirk deepened, the kind of smugness that came from thinking you were the smartest man in the room. I knew I was walking a tightrope, but the thrill of it steadied me—sharp, clear. This was my game, and I was playing him perfectly.

Still, I could feel him.

Booker.

Even with my back partially turned, I knew exactly where he was—across the room, his silent presence as loud to me as a shout. It was like he was watching through the haze of cigar smoke and the low lights, his gaze burning a hole straight through me. I didn't dare look his way. I couldn't afford the distraction, but I knew him too well not to know what he was thinking.

The tension. The fury. The restraint.

Booker always wore his emotions like armor. He thought I couldn't see it—how tightly his fists would curl, or how his shoulders would go rigid when things didn't sit right with him. I didn't need to see him to feel it now. Watching me lean in close to Enzo, hearing the silk in my voice as I spun my lie… it was eating him alive.

Booker wasn't good at hiding jealousy, not from me. And I wasn't naive enough to think this was just about the job.

In his mind, I didn't belong here.

I pushed the thought away, refocusing on the task at hand. The phone. The data. The next step.

But even as I played my part, I knew Booker was sitting at the bar, untouched rum in his hand, his jaw tight and his eyes locked on me. Protecting me. Watching me. Hating every damn second of this.

I needed him to stay exactly where he was—close enough to move if things went sideways but far enough not to blow my cover. I didn't look at him. I didn't need to. But I let myself take comfort in the fact that he was there.

Waiting for my signal.

I leaned forward, resting my elbow on the arm of the chair,

my eyes darting toward the phone Enzo had carelessly placed on the table earlier. The screen glowed faintly before dimming again, its presence taunting me.

It was right there.

So close, yet so damn dangerous.

Enzo's smug grin widened, and I could feel him watching me, taking in every subtle movement like a predator who thought he already had his prey cornered. Men like him—arrogant, egotistical—thrived on feeling superior. I could use that.

"You're not afraid of taking risks, are you, Enzo?" My voice softened just slightly, the tone laced with something more intimate, as if I were peeling back a layer of myself just for him.

He smirked, his chest puffing out a little more. "Life's all about risks, bella. The trick is knowing which ones are worth taking."

I smiled faintly, leaning in a little closer. I wanted him to feel like I was letting him in. Like he had the upper hand. "That's exactly why I came to you. I think we can do big things together, but it's going to require trust. Mutual trust."

Enzo's eyes darkened, the lightheartedness shifting into uncertainty. "Trust?"

I reached forward, my fingers tracing the edge of his phone on the table. Light. Careful. Just enough to make him watch me. "For example—what's stopping me from thinking you'll betray me once I tell you my plans? Or worse, what's stopping you from thinking I'd betray you?"

His laugh was low, more calculated than genuine. "You've got nerve."

I shrugged, letting the faintest smile tug at my lips. "Nerve gets things done. You know that better than anyone." I leaned back in my chair, crossing my legs, deliberately drawing his gaze away from my hand as it hovered near the phone. "How about this—I'll give you my number. Straight access to me. No intermediaries. But you have to trust me first. Trust is earned, after all."

His stare lingered on me for a beat too long, his suspicion giving way to ego. That was the moment. The one where pride makes a man predictable.

Finally, he picked up his phone, unlocked it with a swipe, and slid it across the table toward me. "Fair enough. Put your number in."

I fought the surge of adrenaline that shot through me, reaching for the phone with steady hands. I flipped it in my palm, smooth and natural, as I scrolled to his apps. Just like Donovan showed me, I launched the small transfer tool on my device hidden in my pocket, holding it close enough for the Bluetooth signal to connect.

The phone buzzed faintly against my palm. A vibration no one but me could hear.

Three seconds. Four.

It felt like an eternity as the device mirrored every last bit of data—contacts, messages, calls, files. Everything.

I tapped quickly, entering a fake number in his contact list before handing the phone back to him with a faint smile. "Now we're in business."

Enzo looked down at the phone, nodding in approval. "Smart woman. I like that."

I stood smoothly, fixing the hem of my jacket, already turning away. "Call me, Enzo. I have a feeling this is going to work out for both of us."

Enzo rose, too, following me with his eyes. "I won't keep you waiting, bella."

I didn't look back. Every step closer to the exit felt heavier, like gravity wanted me to stumble. But I didn't.

Out of the corner of my eye, I saw Booker. His fingers curled around his glass and his body rigid. He gave me a nod, those brown eyes burning through me as I walked past.

Time to go.

32

We didn't speak until we were a few blocks away, the muffled thump of Havana's nightlife fading behind us. The car was silent except for the hum of the engine and the faint roar of my pulse in my ears. I gripped the small cloning device in my pocket like a lifeline, the weight of it grounding me.

"Did you get it?" Booker asked finally, his voice low and tight.

I pulled the device out, holding it up. "Every last byte."

"You're insane, you know that?"

I leaned back into the seat, feeling the adrenaline start to ebb away. "It worked, didn't it?"

He shook his head, jaw flexing as he stared straight ahead. "Watching you with him… leaning in, smiling like that—" He stopped, fists clenching briefly before he let them relax. "I didn't like it."

The confession settled in the air, thick and oppressive, like a storm waiting to break. I stole a quick glance at him, noticing how his hands clenched the wheel, knuckles pale against the dark leather. "It was just part of the play," I murmured, my voice barely above a whisper.

His gaze briefly shifted to me, his eyes dark and impossible to read. "Didn't seem like it."

For a moment, I was silent, unsure what to say. I knew what was behind his words, there was storm brewing that I'm not sure that I'm prepared for. I turned my eyes back to the road ahead.

"We got what we came for," I said after a beat, holding the device up again as if it proved my point. "That's all that matters."

Booker didn't answer. He just nodded once, lips pressed into a hard line. But the silence that followed wasn't empty. It was heavy with everything we weren't saying. Everything I wasn't ready to face.

As Booker navigated the winding streets back to the safe house, I stared out the window, the neon glow of Havana bleeding across the glass. My reflection stared back at me—a woman who looked cool, calm, collected. The Queen, back in full control.

But inside, I felt that familiar crack. That jagged edge where the old me and the new me kept colliding.

Booker's words replayed in my head: "Didn't feel like it."

I had no time for his jealousy, for emotions that clouded the mission. But part of me—a part I tried to drown out—wanted to let him in. Wanted to admit how much everything was catching up to me. Bird. Raul. My own reflection in the glass.

I looked down at the cloning device in my hand. Inside it was everything I needed to find Raul. To end this.

But what then?

I pushed the thought away, forcing my focus back to the road.

One step at a time.

33

The kitchen in our new safe house was barely more than a box—peeling paint on the walls, a single dangling bulb that buzzed faintly, and countertops that looked like they hadn't been cleaned in years. But none of it mattered. I had what I needed.

I dropped my bag on the cracked counter, my movements deliberate, but my mind was spinning like a carousel. From my pocket, I pulled out the small cloning device—sleek, matte black, and powerful. I ran my thumb along its edge, my thoughts replaying the look on Enzo's smug face, the way he'd leaned in, so sure of himself. I almost admired how easy he made it. Almost.

Booker was already digging through the fridge. He grabbed two bottles of water, twisted the cap off one, and tossed me the other. I caught it without looking, my eyes locked on the device in my hand.

Booker dropped into a chair in front of me, his eyes never leaving mine. "You think Montgomery's in there?"

"If he's not," I said, my tone flat, "I'll burn Havana to

the ground until I find him."

Booker let out a low whistle, his lips quirking into a faint smirk. "Remind me not to piss you off again."

I shot him a look, but it didn't land like it usually did. I wasn't in the mood for banter. I watched the progress bar inch forward, each percent crawling slower than the last. My pulse thudded in my ears. I wanted to do something—punch a wall, pace the room—but I couldn't. All I could do was wait.

The ping of the completed transfer jolted me like a gunshot. Without missing a beat, I dialed Donovan on the secure line. He picked up before the first ring even finished.

"Mick." His voice was steady, professional, but there was an edge to it—tension from sitting on the sidelines. Donovan might've been in Miami, but I knew him well enough to know this was killing him. He'd never been good at waiting.

"I've got something for you," I said, jumping straight to the point. "Enzo's phone. I cloned it."

"Good work," Donovan replied, the sound of rapid typing coming through the line. "Send it over now. I'll run it through every system we've got and see what shakes loose."

"On it." I hit send, watching the encrypted file upload, the progress bar inching forward again.

"How long?" I asked as soon as it completed.

"It depends on what's in there," Donovan replied. I could hear him still typing, the man already sifting through data. "A few hours at most. But, Mick… this is good. This is real good."

I didn't respond right away, just exhaled the breath I didn't realize I'd been holding. Booker was watching me, his gaze heavy with something I couldn't name. Concern? Frustration? Maybe both.

Donovan's voice softened slightly. "Sit tight, Mick. I'll be in touch as soon as I have something."

"Yeah," I murmured, and hung up.

34

The hours crawled by; the silence between us growing thick, like smog in a room with no windows. I'd paced the floor so long I'd memorized every crack, every squeak beneath my boots. Booker stayed sprawled on the couch, unnervingly calm, flipping a coin between his fingers, the soft clink filling the air.

"You're going to make yourself sick if you don't sit down," Booker muttered, not looking up.

"I can't sit down," I shot.

The coin stilled mid-flip. Booker finally looked at me, one brow arched. I could see it then—the hesitation, the silent questions he hadn't asked yet. He was trying to stay in his lane, but I could feel it brewing under the surface.

The phone buzzed on the counter, the vibration cutting through the quiet like a shot. I grabbed it before it stopped. Donovan.

"You're on speaker."

"You're gonna want to hear this," Donovan said, the sound of furious typing still in the background. "Enzo's phone gave us everything we needed and more—text chains, bank transfers, call logs. It's all there. Raul's been running operations through Enzo's club, but he's not in Havana."

My chest tightened, my heart dropping for just a second.

Booker sat up straighter, his calm demeanor gone. "Where is he?"

"Viñales," Donovan said, his voice sharp. "Private villa. Isolated. Enzo's been covering for him in Havana—running the club while Raul keeps everything quiet at the villa. Drugs, money, weapons. The whole damn thing flows through there."

My pulse quickened, adrenaline shooting through me like a live wire. "Send me the address."

"Already did," Donovan replied. His tone darkened, turning serious. "Listen to me—this isn't small-time. He's got security, men who won't hesitate to pull the trigger."

"I know," I said firmly, glancing at Booker, who gave me a grim nod.

Donovan's voice softened, like he wasn't just talking as my second set of eyes anymore—like he was talking as the man who'd watched me grow up. "Be careful. You're not invincible."

I gripped the phone tighter. "Yeah."

The call ended, leaving silence in its wake.

Booker leaned forward, elbows on his knees, his eyes locked on me. "So, what's the move?"

I hesitated for half a breath before lifting my head, my voice firm. "We go to Viñales."

Booker didn't flinch, didn't blink, but I saw it—the shadow

of hesitation in his eyes. "Mick, hold on. We need to think this through."

"There's nothing to think about," I said, too quickly. "He's there. That's all I need to know."

Booker exhaled slowly, rising to his feet. He turned toward the window, his silhouette framed against the faint glow of dusk outside. "And what happens when you find him?"

"What?" I still my movements and thoughts.

He turned back to me, his gaze piercing in a way that made my chest constrict. "What happens when you get there? What happens when you're face-to-face with him, Mick? What do you want from this—closure? Justice? Revenge? Do you even know?"

His words hit me square in the stomach, knocking the wind out of me. I forced a bitter laugh, stepping away from the table. "Don't psychoanalyze me, Booker."

"I'm not." He stepped closer, slow but steady, his eyes never leaving mine. "I'm asking you a question, Mick. A real one. Because the way you're moving right now? That's not a plan. That's you walking straight into the fire and thinking you'll come out unburned."

"What choice do I have? He played me, Booker! Played with my heart, my name, and my money. You think I'm supposed to walk away? That I'm supposed to let it slide and just—what? Be the bigger person?"

Booker stepped forward, his presence swallowing the room. "No, I don't think you should let it slide. But I don't think you should let it consume you either."

"I don't care!" My voice cracked, raw and uneven.

"You should," he said softly, the calm in his tone somehow louder than my rage. "Because I'm not letting you go through this alone. Whether you like it or not, I'm here."

I glared at him, chest heaving, the weight of his words pressing down on me. "Why are you even here, Booker?"

His face faltered for half a second before he stepped even closer, until he was right in front of me, his voice a low rumble. "Because I'm not leaving you again."

The room tilted. Those words—simple but so heavy—stilled the chaos swirling inside me.

"You don't get to say that," I whispered, my voice trembling. "You don't get to stand here and act like the past doesn't matter. You broke my heart just like this motherfucker did. Just because I had a weak moment and let you in the other night doesn't mean you get to come back so easy."

Booker's jaw flexed, like he was holding something back. But then his voice broke, low and rough. "You think I don't regret it? You think I don't see what I did every time I look at you? Every time you look at me like I'm a stranger?"

I blinked, the anger and hurt lifting slightly.

"I left because I thought it was the only way to save you. And I've hated myself every day since," he reaffirmed, his voice fracturing just enough to crack through my armor. "But I'm here now, Mick. Because I should've been here then. And I swear to God, I'll never leave your side again."

The honesty cut through me like a blade, sharp and unforgiving. I stared at him, the space between us charged with everything we'd never said.

"I don't need you to save me," I whispered, hating how weak it sounded.

His hand came up, thumb brushing along my jaw, his touch unbearably gentle. "I know. You don't need me. But I'm still here. And I'm not letting you carry this alone."

Something in me cracked. My shoulders slumped as the fight drained out of me, and for the first time in years, I let someone else take a piece of the weight I'd been holding.

I leaned forward, just enough for my forehead to rest against his chest, his steady breathing grounding me when my world felt like it was spinning off its axis.

We stayed like that, the silence stretching long and fragile between us. Finally, I stepped back, swiping a quick hand over my face. Booker let me go, but he didn't look away.

"Fine," I said, my voice steadier now. "We go together. But we're not backing down, Book."

"Wouldn't dream of it," he replied softly, a smile playing at his lips.

He held my gaze for a moment longer, then stood. "Then let's finish this. Together."

"Together."

This time, the word didn't feel like a load. It felt like a promise.

"Then we call it a night," Booker said quietly. "We'll figure out next steps in the morning."

For the first time, I believed I could come out of this whole and not just with my power intact, but with something I hadn't realized I needed.

Peace.

35

The safe house was silent. Booker had fallen asleep almost immediately, his soft breathing echoing through the small space. I sat at the kitchen table, a single lamp casting a pool of light across the scratched wood surface. The burner phone sat beside me, silent now, its presence a reminder of the choice I'd made.

I let my fingers trace over the phone's edges as my mind wandered back—back to the years I'd spent running, building walls, and turning my hurt into armor. I thought about Love and how her weakness had shaped me, how I'd promised myself I'd never let anyone make me feel small again. I thought about Hakeem, his indifference burning through me like a brand, and how his idea of love had been control, not care.

And then there was Booker.

The boy who had seen me when I couldn't see myself, who'd been my partner in building our empire, only to walk away. I'd carried the hurt of Havana for so long that I hadn't realized it was less about what he'd done and more about what I thought I'd lost: trust. Connection. Myself.

The faint creak of the floor made me glance toward the hallway. Booker's door was shut, the sliver of light beneath it a subtle reminder that he was close—even if it didn't feel like it. I didn't know what was harder: the silence of his absence or the quiet presence of his unresolved promise to never leave me again.

I slipped the phone into my bag, standing quietly. I needed to step outside, to clear my head. The stifling air inside the safe house felt like it was pressing down on my chest, each moment inside stretching unbearably long. My steps were light as I moved toward the door, the latch clicking softly behind me as I stepped out into the night.

The café was tucked into a quiet corner of Old Havana, its chipped exterior blending into the surrounding buildings. It was the kind of place you could sit unnoticed, a refuge from the chaos just beyond its walls. The scent of espresso mingled with the faint aroma of baked bread, curling through the air like an invitation.

I chose a table in the farthest corner, one that let me observe without being observed. From here, I could see the slow rhythm of Havana at night—the quiet shuffle of footsteps, the faint glow of streetlights, the occasional murmur of voices floating on the breeze.

The burner phone felt heavy in my hand as I turned it over, the edges sharp against my palm. I pulled out the card Agent Cochran had handed me back in that bleak, gray interrogation room. Her name was scrawled in a sharp, clean script, the numbers beneath it a taunting dare.

Raul's face flickered in my mind—his smile disarming, the warmth in his eyes a lie. He had made me feel seen when I was lost, drawn me in with promises that turned to ash. I thought about how I had trusted him, how I'd handed him pieces of myself I hadn't shared with anyone.

But Raul hadn't wrecked me. I realized that now. I'd been standing on unsteady ground long before he came along. He hadn't broken me; he'd just tipped me over the edge.

I dialed the number, my fingers steady as I pressed each button. The phone rang twice before Cochran's voice cut through the silence, brisk and clipped.

"Cochran."

"It's Mickey Collins," I said, my voice firm but calm.

There was a momentary pause, a hint of surprise slipping through before a calm voice responded. "Miss Collins. What's on your mind?"

"I know where he is," I replied simply. "Jason Montgomery. I know where to find him."

The line went quiet for a moment, as if she were trying to gauge my seriousness. "Are you sure?" she finally asked.

"Positive."

I rattled off the location of Raul's villa in Viñales, each word falling from my lips with precision. The scratch of pen on paper punctuated her silence as she took notes, her measured murmurs breaking through the quiet on her end.

When I finished, there was a pause. "How do you know

this?" she asked, suspicion creeping into her tone.

"Does it matter?" I replied evenly. "You wanted him, and now you know where to find him."

Cochran hesitated; her voice softer now "What made you change your mind?"

I looked out the window as a group of children ran past, chasing a tattered soccer ball. Their laughter rang through the streets, a sound so free it felt foreign.

"I just want to move on," I said simply.

She didn't respond right away, and I didn't give her the chance. I ended the call and slipped the phone back into my bag. The chaos in my chest faded, and my heart fell back into its familiar rhythm.

36

The sun had begun to rise, its light spilling over the cobblestones and casting the city in a soft, golden glow. The streets were starting to wake—vendors setting up carts, shopkeepers rolling up their shutters, the hum of morning stretching through the air. I let my feet carry me without a destination, moving through the city as if it could offer me answers I hadn't found yet.

The plazas were quiet but alive, their benches dotted with early risers sipping coffee from small, chipped mugs. Old men hunched over chessboards, their voices low as they debated strategies. Tendrils of cigar smoke curled into the air, adding to the hazy warmth of the morning. I stepped into tiny shops, fingers brushing against polished wooden carvings and delicately woven fabrics. The objects were beautiful, purposeful, but I didn't buy anything. I didn't need to.

As I wandered, my thoughts circled Bird like a vulture waiting for the last scraps of a feast.

Her face was still so vivid in my mind. The pain in her eyes, the sharp edge of betrayal etched into her features. Bird had been more than family to me—she had been my sister, the one who taught me how to walk in heels and keep my balance while running game. She had polished me like a diamond, making me sharp, strong, untouchable. But it had come at a cost—hers, mine, and ultimately ours.

When Bird betrayed me, she didn't just hand me over to Raul. She turned her back on everything we had built together. And in that moment on the cliff, as I watched the defiance and guilt flicker in her eyes, I realized something I hadn't admitted even to myself. Bird's betrayal wasn't just about Raul—it was about her. She couldn't bear being in my shadow anymore, even if it meant destroying the bond we'd forged. And maybe I couldn't forgive her for that.

I told myself her death was justice. But the truth? The truth was murkier than I wanted to admit. Killing Bird hadn't been just about her betrayal; it had been about the part of me that let her get so close in the first place. I hadn't just killed her—I'd killed the version of myself who could have forgiven her.

Maybe that was the price I had to pay. Maybe it always would be.

My thoughts wandered to Harriet—no, Love, as she once insisted everyone call her—as I passed a small café, its bright awning fluttering in the morning breeze. She had been a ghost in my life for so long, a shadow that crept in when I least expected it but always left behind the same scars. Harriet had been broken—a woman who let her vices speak louder than her love, who traded me like currency when the weight of her own life became too much to bear.

For years, I thought I hated her. How could I not? The betrayal wasn't just in what she did—it was in what she didn't do. She didn't protect me, didn't fight for me, didn't choose me. I'd carried the weight of her choices, letting them shape my own armor. But hate was a poison, and deep down, I knew it wasn't just hate I felt. It was longing. The hollow ache of a child who once believed her mother could be more.

I thought about the last time I saw her, standing on that stoop in Brooklyn, her face clearer than I remembered but somehow softer too. She looked… alive. Clear eyes, neatly pressed clothes, hair pulled back in a tidy bun. I had barely recognized her, the woman who now held herself like she was worth something. Like she had finally started believing it. And for a moment, I wanted to believe it too.

But seeing Harriet like that had only deepened the wound. She was someone else's Harriet now—someone else's mother, friend, or neighbor. I wasn't the one she had healed for. I wasn't the reason she had gotten clean, straightened up, found a purpose. It was selfish to want that, I knew, but it still stung.

I wondered what she would think of me now—walking these streets, chasing ghosts. Would she even recognize the daughter she left behind? Would she see the girl she once bartered away, or the woman I'd forced myself to become in her absence? Would she call me out for my choices, for the blood on my hands? Or would she tell me, in that blunt way of hers, that surviving meant making hard decisions?

I envied her in a way I hated to admit. The way she could let the past roll off her shoulders like water, how she could start over and reinvent herself while I stayed stuck in the aftermath. And yet, seeing her like that had planted a seed—something small, fragile, but undeniable. If she could rebuild herself after everything, maybe I could too.

Either way, her face lingered in my mind, a quiet reminder that I hadn't done this alone. Even when I thought I had. She may not have been the mother I needed, but Harriet had shaped me all the same. And now, as I walked these streets, chasing the pieces of my past, I realized that healing wasn't just about what Harriet had done—or what she hadn't. It was about what I could still choose to do for myself.

Hakeem's face surfaced next, unbidden and sharp, the weight of his indifference pressing against me like a steel door. He had been the King of New York once—a legend in the streets, feared and respected in equal measure. But to me, he was just the man the system dropped me with when there was nowhere else to go. My father. The word still felt foreign, like it belonged to someone else, someone who had known what it meant to be loved by him.

But Hakeem Collins didn't love. Not me. He didn't know how. The streets were his only love, and I had been nothing more than an extension of that empire—a pawn in his never-ending game. His love—or what he called love—was always transactional, a balancing act of power and control. I wasn't his daughter; I was his legacy. And for a time, I let him shape me into something I thought was power. I became what he needed because it was the only way to survive.

But survival wasn't the same as strength. Hakeem's lessons were about control, not care. He taught me how to take, not how to hold on. And when he was gone—locked away in a cell with nothing left but his name—I realized how empty his kind of power really was. I had taken over his empire, made it mine, but I never visited him. Never called. Never wrote. I told myself it was because I was busy, because I had an empire to run, but the truth was simpler: I didn't need him anymore.

Even now, years later, his shadow lingered. The choices I made, the walls I built, the way I moved through the world—it all came back to him. Hakeem had planted seeds in me that I couldn't entirely uproot, no matter how far I ran. But as I walked these streets, his voice felt quieter, his presence less suffocating. Maybe that was growth. Or maybe I was finally ready to let him go.

Raul wasn't so different from Hakeem, I realized. The way he used charm like a weapon, slipping under my skin until I couldn't tell where his lies ended and my own hopes began. But the difference was that Raul had been my choice. I had trusted him, believed in him.

But Raul wasn't the architect of my downfall—I was. I handed him the keys. He just walked through the door.

That's why I didn't need to kill him, I realized. Bird had been personal. Bird had been family. Her betrayal cut in ways I wasn't sure would ever fully heal. Killing her had been about survival, about making sure the world knew I wasn't weak, even if it cost me a piece of my soul. But Raul? Raul was just another man who thought he could take from me without consequence.

Turning him over to the police wasn't about letting him off easy. It was about me choosing to let go—of him, of revenge, of the version of myself that needed to make him pay to feel whole. Hakeem had taught me that power was control, that the only way to stay on top was to crush anyone who crossed me. But I didn't want his version of power anymore. I didn't need it.

Letting Raul go wasn't weakness. It was freedom.

For the first time, I felt like I was writing my own story—not Hakeem's, not Raul's, not anyone else's. Mine. And as I walked the streets, the morning sun warming my skin, I let the thought settle over me like a balm.

I wasn't just surviving anymore. I was choosing to live.

The streets grew brighter as I walked, the city's rhythm pulling me along. I wasn't stalling. I was breathing—letting the weight in my chest release, letting the silence hold me for a moment longer.

When I reached the safe house, the early morning light cast long shadows across the walls. I stood at the door for a beat, listening to the quiet hum of the city behind me. I thought of the version of myself who had stepped off the plane in Havana—angry, restless, chasing something she couldn't name. I wasn't her anymore. But I wasn't the girl from New York or Atlanta either.

I was something in between. Something stronger. Something free.

With a deep breath, I pushed the door open and stepped inside, the familiar creak of the wood beneath my feet grounding me in the present.

37

The air inside was cooler; quieter. Booker's voice cut through the silence, low and sharp, coming from the living room.

"Donovan, I need answers. Now." There was a tension in his tone. "She's been gone all night. If she doesn't come back soon—"

"I'm back," I said, stepping into the room.

Booker froze mid-sentence, his head snapping toward me. Relief flashed across his face, followed quickly by something harder to place. He ended the call without another word, tossing the phone onto the couch.

"Where the hell have you been?" he demanded.

I stepped further into the room, setting my bag down on the chipped coffee table. "Walking."

"Walking?" He took a step closer, his brow furrowed. "Mick, you disappeared in the middle of the night. No note, no call—just gone. I thought…" He trailed off, his jaw squeezing. "I thought you went after Raul on your own."

His words hung between us, heavy. The worry in his tone

caught me off guard, making me hesitate before responding. "I needed time to think. That's all."

"Think?" His frustration boiled to the surface, his voice rising slightly. "You don't just walk out without a word when we're in the middle of this. Do you have any idea what was going through my head?"

I looked at him then, really looked at him. The tension in his shoulders, the flicker of fear in his eyes—Booker wasn't angry. He was scared. And somehow, that made it harder to face him.

"I wasn't in danger, Book," I said softly, my voice steady. "I just needed space."

"Space," he repeated, his tone flat. He ran a finger through my hair, exhaling sharply. "You can't do that to me, Mick. Not now. Not after—" He cut himself off, shaking his head. "You don't get to just disappear."

I stepped closer, meeting his gaze. "I know. I'm sorry."

For a moment, we stood there, the air between us charged. His shoulders relaxed slightly, but the tension in his eyes didn't fade. "What happened?" he asked, his voice quieter now.

I hesitated, weighing my words carefully. "I called Cochran," I admitted. "I told her where to find Raul."

His expression shifted, surprise glinting across his face before settling into something unreadable. "You what?"

"It's done," I said, my tone firm. "Viñales. She knows where he is. It's over."

Booker sank onto the couch, his elbows resting on his knees as he processed my words. "You handed him over to the feds," he said slowly, almost like he was testing the weight of it.

"Yeah."

"And you're okay with that?" he asked, his gaze locking onto mine.

I nodded, the decision still settling in my chest but feeling solid. "I am."

He studied me, his eyes searching mine. "Why?"

"Because I'm done letting him take up space in my life," I said simply. "He doesn't get to control me anymore. Not him, not anyone. This was my choice."

Booker leaned back, exhaling slowly. "You're full of surprises, Mick."

I let out a soft laugh, the sound more tired than amused. "Yeah, well, it's been a long night."

He nodded, his gaze softening. "You good?"

I hesitated. Was I good? I didn't know. But for the first time, I felt like I was on my way there.

"I will be," I said finally.

Booker smiled, this time with his whole face, standing and grabbing my hand. "Good. Because we've got a lot to figure out."

"Yeah," I agreed. "We do."

The sun streamed through the window, painting the room in shades of gold. For the first time in what felt like forever, I didn't feel trapped by the walls around me.

38

The morning was quieter than usual, the city's rhythm muffled by the weight of everything that had happened. I stood in front of the cracked mirror in the safe house's tiny bathroom, running my fingers through my hair. For the first time in years, I wasn't putting on the armor of the "bad bitch" everyone expected me to be. No makeup, no perfectly coifed hair, no heels that screamed untouchable. Just me. Mickey. The woman I'd been before the weight of the world made me believe I needed to be something else.

I pulled on a simple outfit—jeans, sneakers, a loose-fitting shirt—and stared at my reflection. The woman staring back at me felt foreign but familiar. I didn't feel smaller or less powerful. I felt… real.

"You good in there?" Booker's voice called from the other room, pulling me out of my thoughts.

"Yeah," I replied, my voice steady. I gave the woman in the mirror one last look before stepping out.

Booker stood near the window, his phone in one hand, a mug of coffee in the other. He glanced up when I entered, his eyes softening as they swept over me. For a moment, he didn't say anything, but the faint smile tugging at his lips spoke volumes.

"You look…" he started, then paused, as if searching for the right word. "You."

I raised an eyebrow. "That supposed to be a compliment?"

"Depends," he said, his smile widening slightly. "Do you take 'beautiful' as a compliment?"

The words caught me off guard, warmth rising to my cheeks despite myself. "You're laying it on thick this morning."

"Just calling it like I see it," he said, his tone light but his eyes serious.

Before I could respond, his phone buzzed in his hand. He glanced at the screen before answering. "Donovan. We're ready. What's the play?"

I watched as Booker listened intently, nodding occasionally, his gaze flipping to me every so often. His calm steadiness grounded me in a way I hadn't expected, and for the first time, I felt like we were moving forward—not just running, but moving toward something.

"Got it," Booker said finally, ending the call. He turned to me, slipping the phone into his pocket. "Donovan's got a jet waiting at the private airstrip just outside the city. We need to move now."

I nodded, grabbing my bag and slinging it over my shoulder. "Let's go."

The drive to the airstrip was uneventful, the city slipping

away behind us as the road stretched into the countryside. Booker's hand rested on the gear shift, his fingers occasionally brushing against mine as the car jostled over uneven pavement. The touches were brief, fleeting, but they felt deliberate—like he was reminding me he was there.

"Everything okay?" he asked, his voice breaking the comfortable silence.

I glanced at him, his profile sharp against the morning light. "Yeah," I said, though the word felt inadequate. "It's just been… a lot."

He nodded, removing his hand from the gear shift and laying it on top of mine. "You got this… We got this."

His words were simple, but they were exactly what I needed to hear.

When we arrived at the airstrip, the jet was already waiting, its sleek frame gleaming under the sun. Donovan's efficiency was almost unnerving sometimes, but today, I was grateful for it. We boarded quickly, the cabin's quiet gentle vibration wrapping around us like a cocoon.

As the jet lifted off, I stared out the window, watching Havana shrink into the distance. Booker sat beside me, his presence a steadying force, though he didn't speak. His hand rested on the armrest between us, close enough to touch but not quite crossing the line.

The sky stretched endlessly outside the window, the clouds a blanket of white beneath us. Booker had drifted off, his head resting against the seat, his breathing slow and even. I envied how easily he could let go, even for a moment.

The jet hummed softly beneath me, a constant vibration that filled the space as I stared out the small window. But my mind wasn't on the view. It was on her.

Harriet. Love. My mother.

Her face came to me like a ghost, overbearing and unrelenting. I could still see her the way she was when I was little—sharp cheekbones, eyes that burned with a fire that could warm or destroy. Back then, I didn't understand what addiction was, only that it took her away from me. That it made her hollow. I didn't know why she traded me for her next fix, why she left me to fend for myself while she disappeared into whatever haze made the world bearable for her.

I used to think it was my fault. That maybe if I'd been quieter, less needy, more of something—anything—she would've stayed. That maybe I could've been enough to make her choose me instead of the drugs.

But the years hardened that pain into anger. Harriet became a name I couldn't say, and Love was a ghost I refused to chase. When child services placed me with Hakeem, I buried her completely. It was easier to hate her than to mourn her. Easier to pretend she didn't exist than to admit how much I missed her. Needed her.

And then I saw her again. It threw me, seeing her like that. For years, I carried this image of her as broken, as incapable. But there she was, defying the story I'd written in my head. It made me angry all over again. Angry that she could pull herself together now, when I didn't need her anymore. When it was too late.

I leaned back in my seat, the leather cool against my skin. My fingers drummed absently against the armrest. Booker adjusts himself in his sleep, his hand brushing mine lightly, grounding me.

I exhaled slowly, letting the agitation roll off me like fog, dissolving into the air. I had finally come to terms and vanished the ghosts of Bird, Raul, and Hakeem, and I didn't want to carry this one anymore. Not Harriet, not the pain, not the bitterness I'd held onto for so long. She is where it all began. It was time to face her, to face myself.

Once we were back in New York, I'd find Harriet. Not to yell. Not to punish. But to close that chapter of my life for good. I needed to know why she had made the choices she did, even if I wasn't ready to forgive her for them. Because running from her hadn't freed me. It had only made her shadow loom larger.

The jet dipped slightly, signaling our descent. I exhaled slowly, the tension in my chest easing just enough to let me breathe.

"Almost home," Booker said softly, his voice low but steady.

"Yeah," I replied, my own voice calmer now. "Almost."

For the first time, going home didn't feel like retreating. It felt like stepping forward. Toward answers. Toward closure.

Toward freedom.

39

The sharp chill of New York air greeted me as I stepped off the plane, its bite cutting through the warmth of my jacket and waking every nerve in my body. The city loomed tall and relentless, as unyielding as it had been the day I left. Its skyline wasn't an invitation—it was a challenge. But this time, it felt different. I wasn't returning to reclaim anything. I wasn't the Queen of Harlem, the bad bitch Mickey fucking Collins, or any of the masks I'd worn to survive.

I was just me. And for the first time, that felt like enough.

The hum of the city swelled as I stepped onto the streets. Cabs honked, conversations buzzed on every corner, and the familiar rhythm of Harlem pulsed in my chest. There was no ceremony, no grand entrance. Just the quiet, steady realization that I was back. Back where it had all begun, and where it all had to end.

I wasn't here to rewrite the past. I was here to bury it.

Brooklyn was quieter than I remembered. The streets here didn't pulse the way Harlem did; they breathed. Slow and steady, like the borough itself had found peace in its chaos.

That same energy seemed to radiate from the small community center tucked between two row houses. Its chipped paint and faded sign didn't diminish its presence—it was a lifeline, a place where broken people came to mend themselves.

And that's where I found her.

Harriet stood outside, her gray-speckled hair catching the soft morning light. Her posture was upright, her movements purposeful. She wasn't the hollow-eyed woman I'd known as a child, the one who disappeared for days, leaving me to fend for myself. She was steady, her edges smoothed by sobriety and time.

It stunned me. I froze, caught between the memory of the woman who had traded me for a fix and the one standing before me now.

She spotted me before I could speak. Her eyes widened, surprise softening into something—hope, maybe, or regret. "Mickey?" she said, her voice trembling, as if saying my name might shatter the moment.

I didn't answer right away. I took a step closer, studying her face. The lines were deeper, her skin weathered by years she couldn't get back, but her hands—her hands no longer trembled. I hadn't known how much I needed to see that until now.

"Can we talk?" I asked, my voice steady.

Harriet's hands twisted nervously in front of her. "Yeah. Of course."

We found a bench nearby, the city's sounds softening into

KITTEN HEELS

the background as the space between us expanded. In that moment, I wasn't a child grasping for her love. I wasn't here seeking her forgiveness. I was here for me.

"I've hated you for a long time," I began, my voice low but firm. "For what you did. For what you didn't do. For not being there when I needed you most."

Harriet flinched, her shoulders curling inward like she wanted to disappear. "I know," she whispered. "I don't blame you."

Her response cut through me. I let the words hang in the air like a cloud before continuing. "But holding onto that hate... it didn't make me stronger. It just made me bitter. I carried it for years, Harriet. Years. And I'm tired. I'm tired of being angry."

She turned to me then, her eyes filled with unleashed tears. "I never meant to hurt you, Mickey. I was sick. And I didn't know how to be anything else."

"I know," I said softly. "And I forgive you. Not for you, but for me. I can't carry it anymore."

Her lip quivered, and the first tear slipped down her cheek. "I don't deserve it," she said, her voice breaking. "I don't deserve anything from you."

I studied her, this woman who had haunted me for so long. I saw her fragility, her humanness, I didn't feel anger or pity... I seen myself

"Maybe not," I admitted. "But you deserve your peace, just like I deserve mine."

Her hand reached out to me, trembling slightly, the gesture

tentative. For a moment, I hesitated. Then, slowly, I took it. Her skin was warm, her grip faint but firm, and in that touch, years of resentment began to dissolve. It wasn't a grand reconciliation. It wasn't forgiveness wrapped in a bow. But it was enough.

"I'm not here to start over," I said gently, meeting her tearful gaze. "I'm not looking for a relationship, Harriet. I just needed to say this. To let it go."

She nodded, her tears falling freely now. "I understand."

And she did. I could feel it, she really did.

I stood, releasing her hand. The weight I'd carried for so long felt lighter now, as if I'd set it down somewhere between her words and mine. As I turned to leave, I paused, glancing back at her.

"Take care of yourself."

"You too, baby," she replied, her voice thick with emotion.

I walked away, my steps steady, my chest rising and falling with a newfound freedom. Harriet wasn't a ghost anymore. She was just a woman. And I was finally free of her shadow.

40

The boutique smelled like fresh linen and gardenias, a signature scent I'd chosen when I opened my first location. I stood near the front window, watching the hustle and flow of Atlanta's Lenox Square. Outside, shoppers moved with purpose, their bags swinging like pendulums, their laughter floating in with every customer who pushed open the glass doors.

Atlanta. It had been my fresh start. I'd come here to escape the ghosts of Harlem, the weight of the streets, the legacy of a name that once meant everything to me. But now, standing here, I realized it wasn't just about escaping. It was about building something that was mine. Something no one could take.

The renovated Fancy Me Boutique was chic, modern, yet warm—a reflection of who I was becoming. No more masks, no more personas. Just Mickey.

The last customer of the day left with a soft chime of the bell above the door. I locked it behind her, turning the sign to "Closed," and leaned against the glass for a moment. The city lights glimmered, casting their glow across the pavement.

Atlanta wasn't home in the way Harlem had been, but it was my sanctuary now. My space to breathe.

"Busy day?"

I turned, startled by the familiar voice. Booker leaned against the counter, one hand shoved casually into his pockets and the other resting on the granite countertop. He was dressed down, his dark jeans and fitted shirt doing nothing to hide his chiseled physique. That same confidence that had drawn me to him all those years ago, but it was the way he looked at me that made my pulse quicken.

"You scared me," I said, but my tone lacked bite. It was hard to be mad at the way he looked at me—like I was the only thing in the room worth seeing.

"Didn't mean to," he replied with a grin, pushing off the counter. He walked toward me, his steps slow as if he was giving me the chance to stop him if I wanted to. I didn't.

"What are you doing here?" I said, folding my arms, though it was more out of habit than defense. I hadn't seen him since we got back from New York, and yet, I wasn't surprised he'd found me.

"Thought I'd surprise you," he said, his tone light, but his eyes told a different story. They were searching, waiting.

I wanted to brush him off, make a joke, anything to hide my nervousness. But I didn't. Not this time.

"Mick," he said softly, his voice tugging at something deep inside me. "How long are you gonna keep pretending we're not still… us?"

I blinked, caught off guard. "What's that supposed to mean?"

"It means I know you feel it. This thing between us—it didn't go anywhere. Let me in."

"Why are you acting like this?" My instincts warring with my heart.

"Acting like what?" His voice rising slightly, though it wasn't anger. It was desperation. "Acting like I love you? Because I do. I always have. And yeah, I messed up. I hurt you, and I'll never stop regretting that. But I'm here now, Mick. I'm here, and I'm not going anywhere."

The rawness in his voice shook something in me. I looked away, my vision blurring slightly as tears pricked my eyes. "You don't know what you're asking," I whispered.

"Yes, I do," he said, stepping closer. He reached out, his fingers brushing against my arm, warm and grounding. "I'm asking for a chance. For us. For what we had—and for what we can have now."

"I don't want to get hurt again." I state trying to push the fear away.

"You won't," he promised, his voice firm but tender. "I'll spend the rest of my life proving that to you if I have to."

The words burst something in me, every fluid in me rushes south. Before I could overthink it, I closed the distance between us, my hands gripping his belt buckle and pulling him in for a kiss. It wasn't soft or tentative. It was years of pain, love, and longing poured into a single moment. Booker's arms wrapped around me, holding me like he'd never let go.

When we finally pulled apart, his forehead rested against mine, both of us catching our breath.

"I love you," he said again, his voice deep and assured. "I love every part of you, Mick. The good, the bad, the edges you think are too sharp. All of it."

I nodded, my tears slipping free, but this time they didn't feel like a weakness. They felt like a release. "I love you too, Book." I finally admit to him and myself as our lips reintroduce themselves while my hands loosen his belt and unbutton his pants.

For this first time in years, I let go, fully. Completely. Allowing myself to love and be loved. Opening my gates, Booker's muscle contracts as his lifts me up in the air and lays me on the checkout desk and mounts me, pressing his full weight against mine.

I am his and he is mine.

Later that night, the boutique's soft lighting bathed the room in a warm glow. Booker's hand trailed over my bare shoulder as we lay together on the couch, tangled in each other. His touch was gentle, but his presence was overwhelming in the best way.

He slowly slid his hand down, intertwining with mine, his thumb brushing over my knuckles. "I've been waiting for this," he admitted. "For you."

"Me too," I whispered, my voice soft.

For the first time, I felt like I could breathe. All the weight of the past—Harlem, Havana, Bird, Raul, Harriet—was lifting, piece by piece. They hadn't broken me. They had shaped me, carved me into someone who could stand in the light without fear.

I turned to Booker, running my fingers along his jawline, memorizing the way his skin felt against mine. "I'm not running anymore."

"Good," he said, his lips curving into a small smile. "Because I'm not letting you."

I laughed softly, leaning into him. As the city lights twinkled outside the window, casting a kaleidoscope of color across the room, I knew this was just the beginning. Not of a new chapter, but an entirely new story. One where I was finally free to be all of me.

With Booker by my side.

EPILOGUE

The house stood on a quiet stretch of coastline, the Atlantic waves lapping at the shore in a rhythm that mirrored Mickey's breathing. She leaned against the porch railing, her fingers tracing the grain of the wood, her eyes fixed on the horizon. The air was alive with salt and the distant cries of seagulls, yet there was a peace here she had rarely known.

Behind her, the sound of laughter spilled out from the house—soft, joyful, and unrestrained. It was the life Mickey had once dared to picture in fleeting moments but had never believed she could truly have. Yet here it was.

Booker stepped out onto the porch, carrying two steaming mugs of coffee. He handed one to Mickey without a word and leaned against the railing beside her. His presence was a steady warmth, as reliable as the rising tide. She glanced at him, catching the glint of the gold band on his finger that matched her own. The life they'd built together was far from perfect, but it was theirs. They had fought for it, scraped for it, and now they were living it.

"You're thinking too hard," Booker said, his voice a low rumble that cut through her thoughts. He sipped his coffee, his eyes studying her with that same quiet intensity she had fallen for all those years ago.

Mickey smirked, shaking her head. "Just taking it all in."

The sound of footsteps brought them both to attention. Their daughter, Camille, bounded onto the porch, her braids bouncing as she clutched a sketchpad close to her chest.

"Mom! Dad! Look what I drew!" she exclaimed, holding up the pad to reveal a crayon masterpiece of the family standing in front of their home.

"That's beautiful, baby," Mickey said, kneeling to examine the drawing. Her heart swelled as she took in the details—the flowers by the front steps, the dog sleeping under the porch, and the glowing sun that framed their little world.

Booker crouched beside her, resting a hand on Camille's shoulder. "You've got talent, baby girl. Keep this up, and you'll be running galleries one day."

Camille beamed, her pride lighting up her face. "You really think so, Daddy?"

"I know so," he said, ruffling her hair before standing and extending a hand to Mickey. "C'mon. Let's hang it on the fridge."

As they headed inside, Mickey's eyes lingered on the photograph sitting on the mantel. It was from Jacob Donovan's announcement rally. Mayor Donovan—now a frontrunner in the gubernatorial race—stood at the podium, his family and closest allies behind him. Mickey and Booker were among them, their support a silent testament to the man who had once saved Mickey from herself.

Donovan had risen far, but he had never forgotten where he came from. His campaign slogan, "For the People," wasn't just a catchphrase; it was a promise. Mickey had seen firsthand how he fought for the forgotten, the overlooked, and the silenced. And while he'd been her protector once, she now stood as his unwavering ally, ensuring that his reach extended to those who needed it most.

Later that evening, after Camille had gone to bed, Mickey and Booker sank into the porch swing, the night enfolding them in its gentle embrace. Above, the stars spilled across the sky in a dazzling scatter of light, each one a reminder of the vastness beyond their little world.

"Do you ever stop and think about how far we've come?" Booker asked, his arm draped around her shoulders, his voice a soft murmur in the stillness.

Mickey leaned into him, her cheek resting against his chest. "All the time," she said, her tone carrying the weight of all they had endured. "It's like we've lived a hundred lives just to get here."

The silence that followed wasn't empty; it was full, brimming with the unspoken acknowledgment of the battles they had fought and the wounds they had healed. Mickey's battles with betrayal, Booker's fight to prove himself, and the chaos they had left behind—all of it had forged them into who they were now. Together, they had built something unshakable.

"You know," Mickey began, her voice thoughtful, "there were nights I didn't think I'd make it. That I'd ever find this."

Booker's lips brushed her temple in a tender, grounding kiss. "Mick, you always had it in you. You just needed to see it."

A smile played at her lips as his words settled over her like a balm. "We're doing more than okay, aren't we?"

Booker's chuckle was low and warm, his hand tracing gentle patterns on her arm. "More than okay," he said.

"We're winning."

The sound of the waves rolling in provided a steady rhythm as Mickey let herself breathe in the moment. Under the canopy of stars, she allowed herself to believe in this life they had created. It was far from perfect, but it was theirs—a future shaped by fire, love, second chances and unyielding determination. A future she had fought for, and one she wouldn't trade for anything.

OTHER BOOKS

BY

KRYS KING

CROSSED IN LOVE

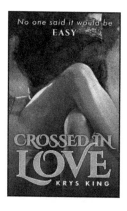

Darcy plays no games when it comes to men.

In her eyes, men are only good for one thing and that is what they carry between their legs. She is a proud mad black woman and likes to thank her fiancé that left her high and dry just months before their wedding for that.

Mickey has heard the story way too many times, she loves her girl but is getting tired of telling her love is money and to hell with all that other mess.

Mickey has never known love and looking at Darcy, she never wanted to. Chante was low-key holding something the other two wanted for themselves and that was family. Chante has the husband and working on a baby, little do her friends know, she is far from having it made, she was holding onto a secret that threatens to destroy everything.

Available now in paperback, and for Kindle®, on Amazon.

THE FRUIT FELL FAR

As First Lady of Alpha and Omega Church of Worship, Kathryn Hill thought she knew how her life would be. But when she catches her husband, Pastor Eric, cheating on her with one of their members, life as she knows it is changed forever. Confronted with his infidelity, Eric claims to be doing God's will. Witnessing the lack of remorse from the self-proclaimed prophet, Kathryn does some dirt of her own. She is soon hit with the reminder of the vows she took on her wedding day by her mother. The words, through sickness and health, through thick and thin, 'til death rang true when Eric collapses during his sermon one Sunday and dies suddenly. When handsome Detective Keith Crane comes knocking on her door, her world is turned upside down when she realizes her husband didn't just die, but was murdered, she's being haunted by a ghost long forgotten, and she is faced with a decision to kill or be killed.

Available now in paperback, and for Kindle®, on Amazon.

ABOUT THE AUTHOR

Krys King is a passionate storyteller and devoted wife and mother of two who has always believed in the power of love to transform lives. A lover of the written word since childhood, she began her writing journey with poetry, many of which were published throughout the years. Writing has always been her outlet, a way to explore the depths of human emotion and connection.

Kitten Heels marks a triumphant return to the literary world as the highly anticipated sequel to her debut novel, *Crossed in Love*. Building on her first two books, *Kitten Heels* reflects her growth as an author, blending her keen sense of storytelling with deeper insights into relatable characters. Five years since her last publication, King considers this her most polished and impactful work to date.

Through Mickey's journey in *Kitten Heels*, King draws

from her own experiences of self-discovery, resilience, and ultimately, finding love—not just in others, but in herself. Her writing resonates with anyone who has ever fought to find their voice and their place in the world.

When not writing, Krys enjoys spending time with her family, diving into love stories of all kinds, and seeking inspiration in the everyday moments of life.

To stay up to date with Krys, please connect with her on social media:

facebook.com/luvvsyc

instagram.com/luvvsyc

www.ingramcontent.com/pod-product-compliance
Lightning Source LLC
LaVergne TN
LVHW040731130325
805874LV00004B/259